The Inner Life of Objects

The Inner Life of Objects

a novel by Maxine Combs

CALYX BOOKS • CORVALLIS, OREGON

The publication of this book was supported in part with grants from the Denison Family Fund of the Oregon Community Foundation and from the Oregon Arts Commission.

With grateful appreciation, CALYX acknowledges the following "Immortal" who provided substantial support for this book:

Nancy Dennis

Cover art: "Still Life" by Gladys Nilsson
Cover and book design by Cheryl McLean and Micki Reaman
CALYX Books Prose Editorial Collective members: Amy Callahan, Margarita Donnelly, Beverly McFarland, Cheryl McLean, Micki Reaman;
Assistant Editors: Amy Agnello, Laura McFarland, Teri Mae Rutledge;
Editorial Assistant: Jessica Mosher.

CALYX Books are distributed to the trade through **Consortium Book Sales and Distribution, Inc., St. Paul, MN, 1-800-283-3572.**

CALYX Books are also available through major library distributors and most small press distributors including Airlift, Baker & Taylor, Banyan Tree, Bookpeople, Ingram, and Small Press Distribution. For personal orders or other information write: CALYX Books, PO Box B, Corvallis, OR 97339, (541) 753-9384, FAX (541) 753-0515.

∞

The paper in this book meets the guidelines for permanence and durability of the Committee on Production Guidelines for Book Longevity of the Council on Library Resources and the minimum requirements of the American National Standard for the Permanence of Paper for Printed Library Materials Z38.48-1984.

Library of Congress Cataloging-in-Publication Data
Combs, Maxine.
    The inner life of objects : a novel / by Maxine Combs.
      p. cm.
    ISBN 0-934971-72-2 (pbk. : alk. paper) : $14.95 —ISBN 0-934971-73-0 (cloth : alk. paper) : $29.95
      I. Title.
PS3553.04794I56   2000
813'.54— dc21   99-36783
                                                                         CIP

Printed in the U.S.A.
9 8 7 6 5 4 3 2 1

Acknowledgments

I'd like to thank the Virginia Center for the Creative Arts for several fellowships. The writing is funded in part by the D.C. Commission on the Arts and Humanities and the National Endowment for the Arts, which provided two individual artist's grants. I'm also grateful to the following people for editorial assistance and support: Jonathan Agronsky, Martin B. Bernstein, Mary Berry, Tom Brewer, Bella Combs, Wayne Combs, Elizabeth Follin-Jones, Karen Green, Faith Jackson, Ann B. Knox, Phil Kurata, Lyn Lifshin, Judith McCombs, Terence Mulligan, Jim Murrin, Betty Parry, Elisavietta Ritchie, Elisabeth Stevens, Tasha Tannenbaum, Hilary Tham.

In memory of my parents,
Sayd Frances Solow and Eugene Maxwell Solow

Part One

FORTY YEARS AGO, as a nineteen-year-old college student, Opal bought a blue dress at a department store. In the dorm, she unwrapped it and saw there'd been a mistake; a black dress lay neatly folded between thin sheets of tissue paper. An hour later, her sister called to tell her of their father's death.

Which meant?

She pondered this question at graveside as shovels of dirt splattered the coffin. She smoothed the black dress that should have belonged to someone else but fit her perfectly. Her father's death (a stroke at age fifty-five) left her with a hundred questions. She looked towards her mother and sister for answers, but their blank eyes foretold they could provide none.

At college again, she shoved the black dress to the back of her closet and forgot it. She majored in drama: *Be an eagle*, Mr. Koldaro, her coach, instructed her. *Better yet be an eagle's egg … as it cracks.* Opal stiffly drew herself up, then collapsed, becoming (in her mind's eye) an egglike ribbon of liquid, dribbling onto the floor. *Observe an eggplant*, he said. *It might prepare you to play Juliet's nurse. Imagine walking like an eggplant. What does an eggplant's smoothness suggest? Its corelessness?*

Opal never became an actress. Actor, Poppy would say. Her egg imitation showed promise, but promise wasn't enough. Also, she didn't want to play Juliet's nurse, she wanted to play Juliet. Though she wasn't the ingenue type. Too tall. Too angular. Voice too dark, too sarcastic, not youthful-sounding. (She was also wrong for Juliet's nurse; if cast in that drama she'd probably play Lady Capulet.) And though she acted in *Macbeth* and *The Skin of Our Teeth* and a few dozen other productions, it turned out she lacked dedication. *Acting is believing*, said Mr. Koldaro, and apparently she didn't believe.

After graduation she waitressed for two years in a coffeehouse, then moved to Washington, D.C., where she spent two years recording tapes for the blind. She was working in a bookstore when the Society hired her.

She enjoyed being a student. She enjoyed being an egg or an eggplant or a Greek queen. She enjoyed options. Forty years later the concept still appeals, although she's forfeited her chance to become someone else.

She's four years older than her father was when he died.

It's Sunday afternoon. If she could choose another identity, who would she be? She can't answer that. If she could choose another locale, where would she be? She can't answer that either, but it wouldn't be here. Not sitting at this desk in what used to be Zach's room, struggling to write a couple of paragraphs. A three-minute introduction that a year ago would have taken an hour.

She stares at the two-and-a-half sentences she's completed: "It gives me great pleasure this evening to introduce Abel Moore. Many of you know Abel Moore's article 'Psychometry and Joshua Quinn,' which appeared in last fall's *Zoetic Review*. His account of finding six thousand dollars ..."

That's it, she's stuck.

Writer's block?

Burnout? She's worked for the Society for almost thirty years. A lifetime. The Zoetic Society. She's brought in their speakers. Edited their review. In the last issue an article on airborne effluvia. An article on the world's first poisonous bird. Four or five articles an issue. Three or four issues a year.

Only two issues last year.

One man in his time plays many parts, Mr. Koldaro said, quoting the bard. *One man?* Poppy would scoff. *What about one woman?* But it's the "many parts" that appeals to Opal, for where is it written that any one thing is forever?

What would Sol say? *Try freelancing? Time to retire?* She'd met Sol in a carpool when she worked at the bookstore. A man who knew obscure alleys and outdoor sculptures. Once an art major, he'd ended up a city planner. *Notice the geometric eagles,* he said, as they sped by an apartment building. *See those parrot gargoyles,* he pointed out as they drove by another.

He'd still wanted to paint and, after they married, although she never changed her name, and after Zach was born, Sol converted the screened porch in the back of the house into a studio. The paintings he didn't sell he stacked in the garage.

The garage!

Don't think about the garage.

Think instead about today's project. During Sol's absence this weekend—he's at his forty-fifth high school reunion and visiting Aunt Rachel—she's been tidying up. A project a day. Yesterday she tackled the cabinet under the kitchen sink. Today she'll clean out two kitchen drawers.

Downstairs, she begins emptying one of them. Why not? Her introduction's going nowhere. No point in wasting time. She removes from the drawer a spatula, a potato masher, an egg beater, three wooden spoons, a ladle, an ice cream scoop, a rolling pin, four cookie cutters, about a dozen skewers. Other gadgets. After ripping out the contact paper that lines the drawer, she wipes it with a sponge and carefully cuts a new sheet of paper to fit into the drawer space. Not an exact match, a little jagged on one end, but close. Next she sorts the utensils, tosses the ones not used in the last year, refills the drawer.

Much better.

She's spent fifteen minutes.

One more drawer to go, which will take another fifteen minutes.

How long would it take to clean out Sol's garage?

She opens the door and surveys it.

Fifteen days?

If something happens to Sol, she'll be the one stuck with disposing of all this stuff. Could she do it? She'd like to try. She'd call one of those "You Call, I Haul" guys who tack their signs up on telephone poles and get him to cart it all away. She'd start with the two defunct floor waxing machines. The chaise lounge with the ripped cushion. She'd wave good-bye to the cracked sundial. The photo enlarger he's been storing for a friend for twenty years. The out-of-commission radiator. The leather suitcase, missing one strap, that looks like it's been scratched by a Tasmanian tiger. The 1984 Epson computer. The cello, out of tune since college.

After the big items are hauled away, concentrate on the smaller ones. Get rid of the carton from the twenty-seven-inch TV, filled with featherless shuttlecocks, old eyeglasses, broken bamboo plant stakes, wooden tennis rackets, a single snowshoe, dead smoke detectors, sprung mousetraps, a never-used fish poacher. Sort through thirty or forty other boxes. What's in them? Who knows? Who cares? One contains wooden hangers. Who needs a box of wooden hangers? Another is filled with old napkins. Who needs any of it?

Toss it all!

She'd keep the phrenological head, balanced on a plant stand and covered by a tattered Stetson.

She'd keep Sol's paintings.

If Sol would stay away two weeks, she'd clear the place out.

Why hang on to two broken floor-waxing machines when no one has ever waxed the floors and no one ever will?

She returns to the kitchen and the second drawer. If he can't impose order, she can. From the drawer she extracts a garlic press, an egg slicer, an apple corer, a meat mallet, a grater, a potato peeler, a whisk, a pastry brush, two sets of measuring spoons, assorted knives.

Since his retirement, Sol paints full time. While she sweats it out at the Society, an organization modeled on the old Society for Psychical Research, but an American version, a local version, founded in the seventies and still operating in the nineties. Like SPR, they chronicle the inexplicable, probe in a scientific manner, keep records.

Document the unlikely.

If God wills it, even a broom can shoot. So says her mother, who admits to no problem with the unlikely, who believes that anything's possible, that the exception proves the rule.

Sol agrees that anything's possible. One day he'll clean up the garage. One day he'll construct a collage from string and mousetraps. One day he'll produce a sculpture from an old radiator that will reveal an odd, absurd life.

Opal removes a church key from the drawer. How long since she's used a church key? Or a tea ball? School reunions and revisiting old neighborhoods not her cup of tea. Aren't her trips to Florida to see her mother, at ninety-two a year older than Aunt Rachel, enough? Sol would say, *Opposites attract. You look to the future, I look to the past.* He'd also say, *You'll finish your introduction. Hang in there.*

Sol manages to be both disorganized and supportive. Once she made a list of Sol's merits, a second list of his deficiencies.

She's a list maker.

Opal empties this drawer, wipes it out, installs fresh contact paper. She should be writing her introduction, but it's stalled. Or is it her life that's stalled? She needs a vacation. A change. If she could will herself into another locale, where would she be? A cypress swamp. Among Mayan ruins. A rain forest. She'd like a church key to punch a hole in her life and allow something fresh to foam up.

She finishes the drawer, and since she can think of no further distracting projects, picks up the issue of the *Zoetic Review* that contains Moore's article, "Psychometry and Joshua Quinn." All weekend she's meant to reread it, but hasn't. She should have read it. She should read it now. She should refold the towels in the linen cabinet. She should become a vegetarian. She should vacuum the venetian blinds.

She's always had trouble with "should."

Indulging herself, she grabs *Borderlines*, an intriguing book she recently discovered at a yard sale. Curled up with it on the sofa, her reading glasses in place, she opens to page seventy-three.

Page seventy-three is as good an entry point as any other. In medias res. As a kid she often entered movies in medias res. Now she turns on the TV in medias res. Enters and exits most situations in life in medias res.

Besides, *Borderlines* lacks a plot. It's a collection of anecdotes. The one on page seventy-three recounts the story of a man from Vancouver who jotted down the name of every single person he met. A lifelong project. His friends from fourth grade. His high school chemistry teacher. A man he chatted with on a bus. Notebooks of names. Thousands of names. Idiotic, but she sees the point. Isn't she a list maker? A list of Sol's good points set against a list of his weak ones. Things to do before the arrival of Abel Moore next Saturday.

The house is quiet, except for the doves under the roof. Their cooings, like wind brushing a tree, the way a shadow might sound, make Opal feel herself in shadow.

She wears jeans and a violet T-shirt, violet to match her aura, which Mona Friendly assures her is violet, although on some days it fades to pink. *Violet because,* Mona says, *you yearn for the Mystic.* Doesn't everybody? Isn't transcendence a universal goal?

She rakes her fingers through her hair. Her curly hair. Curly after fifty-five years of being straight. Thanks to chemo.

At least she has hair. And for that she's grateful.

Why couldn't she have contracted some other disease? Cancer sounds so end-of-the-road. Breast cancer sounds even worse. But here she is. Almost five years later. Alive and reconstructed.

Once she took a cracked plate to be repaired and the restorer gave her three options. *Economy Grade: The repair will probably be visible from a distance of six or eight feet. Medium Grade: The repairs will be visible from a distance of two or three feet, but will not be obvious or offensive to most people. The cost will be two or three times that of Economy Grade. Best Grade: The repair still will not be invisible or like new, but it will be close. We call this Museum Quality Restoration. The cost of Best Grade repair cannot be estimated in advance.*

She'd call her reconstruction Medium Grade. Not Museum Quality, but pretty good.

Unusual to spend the day alone. Sol left early Saturday morning; he should return tomorrow night. She should have read Moore's article, but hasn't. She should have finished her introduction, but hasn't done that either. Instead, she's sitting here, feeling restless. Feeling unfocused. Feeling flawed. Odd that life's delivered her to this exact place at this exact time. Not the place she'd anticipated. It's time for a change, time for her to change. Her life's breaking down. What was that word Geneva mentioned? *Labile*. That's what she is. *Labile*. Breaking down. Unstable. Maybe the agenda of the Society isn't the only imperative. Maybe ...

Can she really be thinking this? For thirty years hasn't the Society figured as Number One?

At her physical exam last month the physician's assistant recorded her height as five feet, six inches. *I'm five-seven*, she insisted and asked him to remeasure. He did, assured her his initial figure was correct, handed her a pamphlet on osteoporosis, and recommended a thousand grams of calcium a day. First breast cancer, then osteoporosis! An inch gone! She could have wept, even though she came out in the ninety-fifth percentile for her age group in stair climbing.

Next she'll refuse to drive at night. She'll pull on a jacket when it's ninety degrees outside—like all the old ladies. Like her mother. She'll tote her toothbrush to restaurants and brush after every meal.

It's five P.M. on Sunday afternoon, the quietest hour of the week. She turns a page in *Borderlines* and finds a spider on it. Where did he come from? Should she kill him or flick him aside? Is he an omen of ruin or rain? Of money coming her way?

Geneva might know.

Better not kill him. She flips him away, grabs her book, and trots into Sol's studio, once the screened porch. A large oil painting sits on the easel. An unfinished oil painting. Its subject is three insects inside a mayonnaise jar. The insects are not recognizable. They don't resemble spiders, not that spiders are insects. They resemble no known creatures. They're odd. Surreal. Two possess women's faces, but the third one's unfinished.

Obviously, there's symbolism here.

Sol feels trapped in a mayonnaise jar?

The garden, visible beyond the sliding glass doors, is nothing more than a brick patio, surrounded by azaleas that have already bloomed. A few fading blossoms still cling to them.

The odor of oil paint hangs in the air. She shoves some rags aside and settles on the mustard-colored sofa. A terrible color, but Sol likes it. This time she opens *Borderlines* to page eighty-five. Here she finds the history of a nineteenth-century baron who solicited "supernatural" messages from statues. Inspired by Moses ("supernatural" writing on the tablets of the law) and by Belshazaar ("supernatural" writing on the wall), the baron left notebooks at the bases of statues so they'd have something to write on. He claimed his method worked and that the messages he received always appeared in the language appropriate to the statue—a note in Russian from a statue of Catherine the Great, a note in French from Napoleon.

Opal closes the book.

One more ridiculous story.

Not addressing the dead directly—as in a séance—but asking the statue of a dead person. People believe the most far-fetched things.

Shark cartilage cures cancer.

Still, it's intriguing.

What would she say to the statue of a dead person? Ask it questions? What questions? What statue? No statue of her father exists, but if one did, that's the one she'd address. Her father who now would be younger than she is. What would she ask him? Should she phase out of her work at the Society? Try for a job editing a government publication? An academic review? If anyone would hire her at age fifty-nine. Ask about Zach? More than a week since she's spoken to him. Is he drifting away? Ask about Sol? Is he drifting away? Is this what happens when you get older? Everyone drifts away.

She doesn't expect specific answers. But a line or two from her dead father would help. Didn't the movie star Ida Lupino receive phone calls from her dead father? Didn't he advise her about a real estate deal? Guide her to hidden, important papers?

Anything's possible.

She stares at Sol's painting. If she left a notepad by the third insect? The unfinished one, unfinished like her father's life. If statues can write notes, why not a figure in a painting? Maybe it will give her some tips.

Absurd, but she finds paper and pencil and places them next to the insect painting.

Now, down on the floor, she assumes a half-lotus posture. Begins to breathe. When you breathe, you inhale the universe. When you breathe, your mind steadies and calms. In this posture, eyes slits, tongue pressed against front teeth, she concentrates on her breath arising from her chest. Slowly, the flow of her thoughts enters the daubs of paint. As she inhales, she counts to four, holds the breath as she counts to seven, exhales as she counts to eight.

Five times she repeats this pattern.

After three minutes she opens her eyes.

It's up to the figure now.

"LAST NIGHT RUSSELL asked me to marry him." Poppy plucks a brown frond from the Boston fern on her desk.

"Russell!" Opal looks up from the copier. Russell? Poppy's been volunteering at the Society for only a few months, but during that time several boyfriends have surfaced. A lawyer who became a baker. A computer wonk. Tough to be twenty-three. Tough to have so many boyfriends it's confusing.

"Botanist," Poppy prompts. "Red hair."

Opal pushes the copier's start button, but nothing happens. A memory flickers. A young man who stopped by the office one day carrying an armful of branches. Specimens for a lecture he was scheduled to give. Like Birnham Wood. "What did you say? Did you accept?"

Poppy tamps dirt in the fern's pot. "I said I'd think it over. That I'm not sure. That I'm not prepared to give up my independence."

"I didn't think women gave up their independence these days." Opal opens the copier to check for a paper jam. She hopes she doesn't sound like a grandmother.

Poppy's mouth twitches. "I believe I have a mission in life, although I don't know what it is. If I get married, I may never find out."

"You make marriage sound like being kidnapped by UFOs." Opal shakes the machine as if a rearrangement of its parts will solve its problem.

"Good analogy," Poppy concedes with a little smile and unwraps a cheese sandwich.

It's Monday noon in the Zoetic Society office, two rooms on the second floor of a small Takoma Park building. The office is in a mixed neighborhood, a deli next door, a dress shop that's going out of business next door to that, a secondhand bookshop across the street. Downstairs from the Society there's a stationery store, and upstairs there's the office of a man who keeps his occupation a secret.

Poppy, a thin, pretty girl, is dressed this morning in a white polo and khaki pants. She wears a garnet ring on her right hand and two earrings in each ear, a diamond stud and a large gold hoop. Her fair hair is pulled back in a ponytail. To Opal she looks as normal as the girl next door, except that the line of her mouth is a little too tight.

Opal abandons the defunct machine along with her common sense. "Do you love him?" she asks, crossing her fingers the question won't be taken the wrong way. Won't seem too personal. She likes Poppy, thinks Poppy likes her, and wants to keep it that way.

The phone rings.

Poppy answers. It's her mother. Opal picks up a magazine and pretends not to listen, impossible in an office this size. Poppy's mother does most of the talking, Poppy most of the listening.

What Opal overhears is that Poppy doesn't mention Russell's proposal to her mother.

Why is that?

Easier to talk to strangers?

Not that she's a stranger. In the few months Poppy's been with the Society, Opal has picked up the major headlines if not every supporting detail about her young coworker.

She knows there's a failed romance in Poppy's past.

She knows there's a child: Metro. Named after both Demeter and the train.

She knows Poppy's "into" the goddess.

She knows that Poppy discovered the Society in a peculiar way. One Tuesday night while eating at Chadwick's with her mother, a piece of flank steak stuck in Poppy's throat. The man at the next table rushed over and performed the Heimlich maneuver. This effort dislodged the meat and saved Poppy from choking. Later, the man let slip that he usually ate at Chadwick's on Wednesdays, but for some reason had come a day early.

He'd come a day early to save her!

This incident confirmed Poppy's belief that a Higher Power had singled her out, and the next day she looked under "psychics" in the yellow pages, found a listing for the Society, and began coming in to learn more about that Power.

Also from that day, Poppy stopped eating meat. A piece of steak had caused the problem, hadn't it?

Opal, who'd like to become a vegetarian but has never found the willpower, starts her lunch of cold chicken and celery sticks. She plugs in an electric kettle for hot water.

After the phone call, Poppy returns to her sandwich. "How can I marry?" she asks, sidestepping the question of love. "The world's screwed up. Men earn thirty percent more than women for comparable work. Men speak up forty-five percent more in classrooms than women do."

"Don't trust statistics," Opal recommends. "Numbers can be twisted to support any point of view."

"A woman's more likely to be the victim of a terrorist attack than to marry after age thirty."

Opal crunches a stalk of celery. "Myth. No more true than that the sewers are filled with alligators. Or that sending pull tabs to a certain address will buy dialysis time for a kidney patient." Opal feels on solid ground now, the swampy footing of her personal relationship with Poppy no longer the issue. This is what she's good at. What she's dedicated her life to. Figuring out what's true, what's false, what's relevant. Not that Poppy should worry even if her last statement were true. She's only twenty-three. And Russell's isn't the first marriage proposal she's mentioned in the three months she's worked at the Society.

"Besides," Poppy throws in, "even in marriage, the average couple spends less than four minutes a day in conversation."

When Geneva Lamb, the other volunteer, arrives, Poppy's brushing away crumbs and Opal's chewing a chicken wing. Geneva carries a plastic box of salad from the deli next door.

Geneva's a tall young woman in her early thirties whose crinkly hair reminds Opal of parsley. She's dressed oddly: ankle-length skirt with a pattern of tiny roses on it; a wrinkled, made-in-India, white gauze blouse; a knitted mauve vest. She could pass for a flower child from the sixties, except for her combat boots. And her expression. Her expression doesn't fit the flower child stereotype. It's not wide-eyed and innocent enough. Elfin enough. Instead, her expression suggests a preoccupation with higher matters.

Opal watches Geneva drift towards her desk—in spite of the boots—as if she's groping through a fog. She worries that she'll knock over the wastepaper basket.

Poppy reaches out a hand to protect the coat rack.

"Greetings," Geneva says. She arrives—without knocking anything over—at her swivel chair and fishes inside her lopsided striped straw handbag for a can of Diet Coke. She pulls the tab and announces, "I heard on the radio that a vision of Eleanor Roosevelt appeared on an old Formica tabletop in a city dump."

Poppy sniffs as if Geneva's just dragged home a dead bird to show it off.

Opal straightens her back. "A vision of Eleanor Roosevelt! What city?"

"Houston. They've built a shrine, and hundreds have started bringing flowers and burning incense."

Opal crumples a napkin around her chicken bone and tosses it into the wastebasket. Eleanor Roosevelt on a tabletop. A possible story for the *Review*? What will people dream up next? Florence Nightingale in a birdbath! Madam Blavatsky in an ice cube tray! But back to Eleanor. "City dump. Tell me all."

"It started as a glow, then changed into a face."

Opal takes a few notes.

Geneva pops open her plastic salad box. "Probably an optical effect."

"Optical effect's a cop-out explanation," Poppy complains, her glance resting on Geneva's unevenly cut fingernails. "Some people explain the Yellow Blob that way. Or UFOs."

Geneva raises an eyebrow as if the gesture were force enough to disintegrate the Yellow Blob. As well as any stray UFOs. Why are you so gullible, the eyebrow seems to ask. The tall young woman returns to her salad and spears a chunk of tomato with her plastic fork. "According to the newscaster, the 'image' appears in a triangle of light with a blue border."

"What station?" Opal asks.

Geneva provides name of the station, name of the newscaster, time the report aired.

Opal jots it down, keeping in mind that Geneva doesn't believe a word of it.

Geneva's also a recent addition to the Society. Another volunteer. But Geneva didn't sign up because she believed a Higher Power chose her. Geneva doesn't believe in Higher Powers. She's made it clear she's never had a paranormal experience and that she doubts anyone else (especially Poppy) has had one either. She admits that she's superstitious, believes her itching nose means a letter, but swears she's not the kind of person who "sees" things.

Instead she's a scholar. Opal has seen her dissertation, bound in black leather. A Yeats scholar. After she finished her classwork, Geneva joined the Society because she hoped that belonging to a group investigating the paranormal—Yeats belonged to several such groups—would improve her critical skills. Inspire her to greater insight. Transform her into a more sensitive literary critic.

That's half the story. The other half is that Geneva joined the Society in a desperate attempt to change her life.

Her life had fallen into a terrible rut. She'd put all her eggs in the academic basket. This strategy landed her a dissertation and a degree, but no boyfriend, no job, no social life. Like the birdman of Alcatraz, she'd given the best years of her life to research. Worse yet, she'd constructed the prison walls herself, term paper by term paper. Now she had to dismantle them. She had to! Better late than never. She joined the Society. Enrolled in an exercise program. Started sampling a new restaurant once a week. Tried to write a children's story. Put away her critical texts and picked up some detective novels.

Opal brews green tea. She hands a cup to Poppy and one to Geneva, both young enough to be her daughters, yet different as night and day. Geneva smart, but inept. Didn't she confide that once she served guests a platter of raw shrimp, not realizing she needed to cook them? And Poppy. Pretty, normal-appearing Poppy, but awaiting divine instruction, a la Joan of Arc.

They coexist. They tolerate each other. At times more than that. Poppy seems to admire the single-mindedness that Geneva hopes to abandon. She likens Geneva to Atalanta, a chaste, brainy competitor, someone who can win the race. Therefore she forgives her her odd clothes and superior attitude, her unkempt fingernails.

And Geneva romanticizes Poppy. Poppy who's loved and lost. Poppy who's raising a child on her own. Poppy who's always got a boyfriend.

The afternoon slips away. Poppy designs a flyer advertising Abel Moore's upcoming lecture. Geneva opens and answers mail. One letter inquires if an article on mazes would be suitable for the *Zoetic Review*.

Geneva hands the letter to Opal. "Mazes. Anfractuous designs."

Opal and Poppy exchange glances.

Poppy reaches for the dictionary. *Anfractuous. Characterized by intricate turnings or windings* …

Opal files the letter, telephones about the malfunctioning copier. Later, she picks up the issue of the *Zoetic Review* in which Moore's article appeared. The magazine opens to a piece on "the lumpy rug syndrome," defined as "the tendency to shove under the carpet inexplicable concepts." She finds Moore's article, paperclips the page, but sets the magazine aside.

Five days till Moore's arrival, the dinner at Mona Friendly's, the rest of it. A hundred things to do. Can she do them? So far she's neither reread Moore's article nor written her introduction. These realities don't change by the time Poppy leaves at four P.M. or by the time Geneva leaves at five. Geneva lives in the neighborhood, doesn't own a car, and announces she plans to stop at an Indian carryout for dinner. She mentions that her nose itches and that she's hoping for a letter.

Opal remains after her coworkers leave. Sol won't be home until ten or eleven, no reason to hurry. It's pleasant being alone in the office. Just like the old days. The *Review* a simple newsletter then. The office a ratty room in Silver Spring, still a big step for the dozen people who started out at Dr. Wescot's to discuss "dreaming true." Or was it "spirit photography"? Some such topic. Maybe eighty members when they moved here—in the middle of a blizzard. Can twenty years already have passed? Mrs. Corinth with her hot cider at those early meetings—dead now—leaving behind her hundreds of books that now fill the library shelves.

Opal stares out the window but sees nothing. She's inside her head. Eleanor Roosevelt in a city dump. Poppy believed it, Geneva didn't. What would Sol say? *If you believe it's there, it's there.* What would the figure in Sol's painting say? The one she left the memo pad next to. So far—she checked that morning—no message has appeared. She'll look again this evening. Would Zach buy the Eleanor Roosevelt story? Probably not. She straightens her back. A three-minute introduction that a year ago would have taken her an hour.

Shadows fill the street outside.

At seven P.M. she hears a door close on the third floor. The mystery tenant leaving for the day. George Bluestone. Who is he? What does he do? He carries a leather briefcase but keeps what inside it? An unidentifiable aura emanates from him. He could have spent his boyhood in Tahiti or he could be a stranger on a train. His mailbox downstairs reveals his name but not his occupation. The frosted panel in his office door is blank.

Although he's been up there a year, Opal's never seen a visitor enter his office. A month ago, when she met him on the landing outside her door, she positioned herself to block his path up the stairs. "I'm Opal Kirschbaum," she said before he could maneuver around her. "I run this office." She waved a hand at the door behind her. "I don't know whether you're interested in psychic phenomena or not, but if you are, come to one of our meetings. The next one will be Tuesday, and we'll be talking about the hundredth monkey phenomena."

George Bluestone shifted his briefcase. He was a tall, worried-looking man, with round steel-rimmed glasses and brown dishevelled hair. "Opal ... what an interesting name." Then he added, "I'm afraid I'm occupied on Tuesday."

"Too bad. We meet regularly. I'll slip a schedule under your door, and—"

"Thanks very much."

Opal, unable to ignore George Bluestone's impatience, threw out a little wildly, "My coworkers have been taking bets on what you do up there."

George Bluestone half-smiled. "I'm afraid I don't fit the usual categories." He shifted his briefcase again, and Opal reluctantly moved aside.

"See you around," she called, as he mounted the stairs.

No response.

The next day she slid a schedule of the upcoming meetings of the Society under his door, but he neither acknowledged her gesture nor found his way to any subsequent meeting.

"Unfriendly," Opal concluded as she described her encounter to her coworkers.

"He doesn't sleep there," Poppy noted. "He seems to be his own boss."

"Unfriendly," Opal repeated.

Geneva expressed no opinion.

"Maybe he's rich," Poppy speculated.

The women discussed their upstairs neighbor but established no certainty about him. Meanwhile he came and went, received no visitors. He seemed like a dangling wire. Awkward—perhaps harmless, perhaps dangerous.

Still, on that May evening, after she locks the office door, Opal walks up a flight and slips one of Poppy's flyers under George Bluestone's door.

POPPY PICKS HER son up at day care and drives to their Glover Park apartment. The kitchen sink has a rust stain around the drainage hole, and a wobbly ledge over the kitchen window supports an African violet, a geranium, and a spider plant.

Poppy slides two frozen macaroni and cheese dinners into the oven, waters her plants, switches on the TV for Metro, settles onto the sofa, and reaches for the book she's been reading: *A History of Women in America*. Other books within reach are *The Great Mother: An Analysis of the Archetype*, *When God Was a Woman*, *Women's Mysteries: Ancient and Modern*, and *The Great Cosmic Mother*. What's more crucial than reading? Didn't reading teach her about Isis? Isis who said, *I Isis, am all that has been, that is, or shall be.* Isis who assumes a thousand guises. Demeter. The Green Goddess of Earth. Queen of the Heavens. Fortuna, Goddess of Good Fortune.

Eleanor Roosevelt on the tabletop no doubt another manifestation.

A History of Women in America informs its readers that in the 1830s only seven occupations were open to women but inexplicably fails to specify which ones. Did the author lose focus? Assume her readers knew the seven occupations the way some people know the seven deadly sins? School teacher? Milliner? Seamstress. Poppy folds over the top corner of the page. Maybe Opal or Geneva can complete the list.

The book argues that the invention of the typewriter created a profound impact on women's lives. In the 1870s, ninety-five percent of secretaries were men, but by 1900, seventy-five percent were women.

Don't trust statistics, Opal counseled.

But statistics lend weight.

At dinner she adjusts the tray on the two-year-old's highchair. "Today only twenty-one percent of women classify themselves as homemakers, as compared with fifty percent thirty years ago." Never too early to begin a child's education.

"Percent," Metro parrots and waves his cup of milk.

"Today, twenty-one percent of lawyers are women, as compared with three percent thirty years ago."

Metro waves his cup more vigorously.

"Spill that and I'll feed you to the typewriter." If only Metro were five years older and capable of real discussion.

"Typewriter!" Metro shouts.

"Eat your dinner." She points at his aluminum tray of macaroni and cheese. "Would you like to stay with GiGi on Saturday?" Gigi is Metro's name for her mother.

"GiGi!" Metro crows.

Good! He'll go to GiGi's, and she'll be free to attend Abel Moore's lecture. What will she discuss with the great man if she gets the chance? Ask questions? Are there such things as disappearing stars? Can a person's eyes actually give off light? What will he be like? A man who finds what's missing. An author. Older. Grey-haired. Attractive?

Later, after Metro's had a cookie, a bath, and fallen asleep, she rearranges his quilt and bends to kiss him. Thank God, he's asleep! Finally! She'd wanted a girl, but Metro's beautiful. Olive complexion. Dark lashes. Dark hair. No resemblance to herself.

Exactly like Vic.

No need to waste time thinking about Vic.

Back to A History of Women. Typewriter, vacuum cleaner, sewing machine—appliances that altered the lives of women.

She could sign up for Women's Studies. What exactly do they study in such programs? Learn about The Seneca Falls Convention? The Triangle Fire? Read Kate Chopin?

She could relocate and start a new life. Except for Metro, her present life isn't working. Maybe Abel Moore will invite her to Florida to work at his institute. She might do it.

Why not?

Still no need to work.

Thanks to Amtrak.

Amtrak, the birth of Metro, her rescue at Chadwick's—the milestones of her adult life.

Amtrak came first.

That not-to-be-forgotten crash. She'd been returning from a weekend in Syracuse when the jolt occurred. It felt like a boulder smashing into them. Or another train. As the brakes screeched and whistles shrilled, screaming passengers were flung from their seats. A voice shouted, "We're off the tracks!" More screaming. Four dead on the spot, dozens injured, the engineer, it turned out, high on pot. Driving under the influence. Later, she visited a psychiatrist for trauma. Later still, became a claimant in a class action suit that eventually got settled.

She's been living off the money ever since. She didn't get killed and Amtrak is paying her. Proof positive that Divine Providence is on her side. First the money, then the birth of Metro, then her rescue. As if a plan were unfolding.

She can finish her undergraduate degree in two years if she puts her mind to it. Then what? Law school? But is her brain a law school brain? Doubtful. She can't even sit still for Perry Mason reruns. Study geology? Underground layers interest her. Open a bookstore? Nothing more important than reading. Work in a florist shop?

Some place must exist for her.

Why can't the plan that's unfolding be a little clearer? Drop a hint what her next step should be. Speak to her as Eleanor Roosevelt's face speaks to the citizens of Houston. Should she teach school? Elementary school or high school? She can do most things as long as they don't require mechanical skill. But even simple mechanical acts confound her. Impossible to figure out how to open any spray bottle or operate the shower in any strange bathroom.

Vic has mechanical ability.

But no point thinking about Vic.

Cooking is also beyond her. Nor does she know the names of trees. She'd like to know them. Russell knows them.

She met Russell at the National Arboretum where she'd taken Metro to see the oversized goldfish. Koi. A tall young man with red hair strolled by carrying a deck chair—a deck chair at the arboretum?—a young man with an outdoor aura to whom she directed a question. She was curious, she was bored, how long can you look at goldfish?

He put the chair away, explained that he worked there, and invited her and Metro to tour Fern Valley. She admired the bloodroot, the jack-in-the-pulpits.

Now he wants to marry her.

He doesn't know she can't cook. The word "bride" derives from the Teutonic word "to cook," according to one of her books. A few other details Russell doesn't know. He doesn't know about her rescue, he doesn't know she's divinely protected, he doesn't know she considers reading all important.

He doesn't know about Vic.

The phone rings. It's her mother who agrees to take Metro on Saturday and advises Poppy to get a haircut before Abel Moore's lecture. Poppy's mother believes a good haircut is the key to most professional and social occasions.

Poppy smoothes her hair away from her face and promises to think about it. Mrs. Greengold also feels Poppy should move back home.

Everyone has a plan for her.

But she wants to forge her own path. Figure out what she needs and what she believes in. She believes the Goddess is the author of all being. The Righteous Judge. The Bestower of Strength. She believes in psychometry. She believes that Eleanor Roosevelt's face appeared on the tabletop.

Geneva disbelieves in the face in the tabletop. She said it could be an optical effect. She believes in English literature.

Opal considered the face a possibility. She mentioned other face stories. Faces etched in windowpanes. Faces in rock formations. Faces in damp stains on walls. She brought up those drawings for children where you search for hidden faces. She used the word "simulcra" and said each case warrants individual investigation.

Opal keeps an open mind.

Simulcra. Poppy looks the word up in the dictionary. *Plural of "simulcrum." Image, usually insubstantial. Unreal semblance of a thing. Shadow.* A shadow face? Attached to a shadow man? What was that syllogism they studied in Philosophy 101? *All men are mortal. Socrates is a man. Therefore Socrates is mortal.* What about all women? Why are women always left out? *All men are created equal.* Here, *men* (so they say) encompasses women. The phrase, *Early man*, refers (so they say) to the species. But why can't you say, *Man is the only animal that menstruates?* Would this be the kind of incongruity studied in Women's Studies?

It's 9:30. If she marries Russell … she's twenty-three, it's the nineties, what's the hurry? Why get stressed? Why marry someone because he knows the names of trees? When Russell calls at ten P.M., which he usually does, she'll say she needs more time.

This is what she does. But once he's on the phone, she invites him to Abel Moore's lecture.

"A psychic?" he says, doubt in his voice.

"A psychic."

"I'm leading a trip to Dyke's Marsh Saturday afternoon—"

"The lecture's at eight."

"You think I'll like it?"

"This guy can tell about a person just by holding his penknife. He senses vibrations."

A moment of silence, then, "Okay. Try anything once."

The conversation drifts. Poppy considers telling him about Isis, the Giver of Life, but decides not to press her luck. She does tell him about the face in the tabletop. He tells her about an outbreak of "white rust" that's threatening chrysanthemum nurseries around the country.

They make a date for dinner the following night.

IN THE INDIAN carryout Geneva notes three tables, the long counter in back, the cooler along one wall, the tape of reedy-sounding music. She studies the menu board suspended over the counter and orders Chicken Kadai without knowing what it is. Time to live and learn.

She sits by the window.

Last week it was Pad King in a Thai restaurant. The week before Doro Wat, an Ethiopian dish so hot she required two Diet Cokes. Every week, a new dish; that's her ambition. Haul herself out of her rut, broaden her horizons, experience life not through books, but directly.

Chicken Kadai turns out to be chicken in what tastes like a curry sauce. Of course, "curry" doesn't exist; it's a blend or a mixture, but a mixture of what? Coriander? Ginger root? A thickening agent like flour? Slivers of onions and green peppers float in the stew, plus other unidentifiable chunks. Another bite convinces her to get a soda from the cooler. She adjusts her long legs under the table, eats slowly, sips the Diet Coke.

The table's Formica top, white with gold flecks, displays no face. No Eleanor Roosevelt. But only the disturbed see faces in tabletops. Or the visionaries. Yeats once saw a Titan rising from the desert. Not a face in a tabletop, but the same order of event. Blake saw angels sitting in the branches of trees.

This Chicken Kadai's not bad.

A couple at the next table bend over plates of skewered meat. The girl has a heart-shaped face and the young man wears striped South American pants. He says, "I had soup for lunch today and burned my tongue." The girl replies, "I only eat two meals a day and lunch isn't one of them."

It's still light when Geneva leaves the restaurant. As she walks home she keeps an eye out for rough spots in the pavement and potholes. What causes potholes? Cold weather? Abrupt changes in the weather? She has a Ph.D. but most simple facts elude her.

The sun's low and radiant. Late afternoon's the best time for photographing buildings, but why is that? Because the angle of sunlight softens them? Highlights them? She can define postmodernism, but knows nothing about angles of sunlight. A shame, because it's amazing what happens to buildings against a late afternoon golden sky. They seem glorified. The dry cleaners, the wedding dress shop, the bookstore; a fire seems to transfigure them all.

A dangling tree limb catches her attention. It could fall at any minute. She jots down its location in the small notebook she always carries.

Her house, a rented bungalow, is shabby. It needs work. A paint job, then repairs to the crumbling front steps—like the tree limb they could fall at any moment—and the straggly azaleas in front should be cut back. But what's the point? She's a renter; she's almost out of here; all she needs is a job and she'll be on her way. Until then, mind over matter is her motto.

The mail's a bust. So what did her itching nose mean? Only an advertising flyer, some dollar-off coupons from the supermarket. Not *the* letter. Three weeks ago she wrote letters to sixty schools, applying for teaching jobs. Sixty letters and so far not one response. She wrote to every university and junior college in the area, but she'd settle for Alabama or Alaska. Sell what's too heavy to move and ship the rest. At thirty-one, she wants a job. She wants a letter that begins: "Dear Dr. Lamb: We read your recent letter with great interest as we do anticipate an opening in Twentieth-Century British Literature next fall. Would you be available for an interview ..."

She'd be on the next plane.

How am I fallen from myself, for a long time now
I have not seen the Prince of Chang in my dreams.

Yeats quoting a Chinese poet.

That's her problem. She's fallen from herself. She's disconnected from the life she led before grad school. All those years of reading, reading, reading. Those years of hibernation. A job will reconnect her to the world.

Besides a job, a boyfriend would help. Like the girl with the heart-shaped face in the carryout who eats only two meals a day has. Like Poppy has. Someone who listens to her. Someone with whom she's at ease. Someone interested in her eating habits. If only she weren't such an Amazon.

At five feet, eleven inches, she's been slouching since seventh grade.

She once wrote a paper on Amazons that noted that in prehistory Amazons ruled much of Asia and North Africa, that until the fifth century, the Black Sea was called the Amazon Sea, and that Amazons tamed horses and could marry only after they'd killed three enemies.

She'd like to marry, but not to kill three enemies. Not that she has three enemies, and, knock on wood, she intends to keep it that way.

She bends to thump the wooden floor.

Besides Amazons, she identifies with mermaids. That's because she's a swimmer. Of course, Amazons existed and mermaids didn't (and don't), any more than that apparition of Eleanor Roosevelt exists. Still, water creatures appeal. She likes to read about them. The most interesting category of "paranormal event" has got to be water monsters. The Loch Ness Monster. Ogopogo. Captain Haslefoot's Sea Serpent.

When she mentioned mermaids at the office, Opal, the fact collector, remarked: "In the nineteenth century, the British claimed that all mermaids found in British waters belonged to the crown." And Poppy, predictably, put in: "Mermaids are associated with Aphrodite, who arose from the sea. They're a form of the Goddess."

The only items in Geneva's living room are a forty-five-inch TV and a treadmill. A year ago she tossed out the sofa and other furnishings, promising herself if she watched TV, she'd simultaneously exercise. Kill two birds with one stone. But she doesn't feel like exercising at the moment, so she turns on the TV and watches standing up.

During the weather report, Brenda Lovejoy, her next door neighbor, arrives and asks to use the phone, since her own lacks a dial tone. Brenda's a short woman of fifty, with direct sympathetic eyes. She's a nurse.

She holds up a calling card. "Could I make a quick call to Indiana?"

"Sure." Geneva gestures towards the phone knowingly, even though she has no idea how to use a calling card. She doesn't even own a credit card. She's been studying so long that she's never learned how to use these instruments of modern life.

Brenda dials but gets no answer.

She hangs up and pockets her charge card. "My nephew Peter's coming to visit, and I hoped to talk to his mother. My sister. I haven't seen Peter since he was eleven."

"How old is he now?"

"About twenty. Any idea what I should do with him when he's here? I'm not used to twenty-year-olds."

Geneva reflects for a moment, then offers, "We're having a psychic speak at the Society on Saturday night."

"A psychic! Does he tell the future?"

"He reads the life of objects."

"It's a thought. I'll ask Peter when he comes."

Later, Geneva reads her murder mystery. When she gets sleepy, she climbs into bed which is on a north–south alignment (to facilitate sleep) and turns off the light.

AT HOME OPAL checks Sol's picture for a message. Nada. The pad's blank. Next she leafs through her mail. A catalogue that advertises classes in "Understanding Your Inner Child," "Yahweh Power," "The Mysteries of Lemuria." Ads for "organic burritos," "crystals," "astro-chemical analysis."

So many hoping to activate their undeveloped powers. Yet the Society's membership has dwindled. At their peak, they enrolled 125 members; now only thirty-five find their way to meetings. Some dropped out, others took up New Age activities: channelling, drumming, self-hypnosis. Opal distrusts this trend; New Age rhetoric sounds thin to her. Not like the Society. Here, no one pretends to answers. Instead they investigate. If Eleanor Roosevelt's face shows up on a tabletop, they don't just accept it. If only she had a dollar for all the apparitions the Society has investigated: lake creatures, mystery clouds, monkeys with lions' heads, Chinese wildmen, phantom boatmen, aliens, Men-in-Black, UFOs, pink frogs, artifacts from Atlantis excavated while constructing a Hardee's restaurant.

It requires a sense of humor.

And the Virgin Mary. Sighted hundreds of times a year. Worldwide phenomena. In Uganda she promised to find a cure for AIDS; at a Pennsylvania summer camp she shed tears. In Venezuela she appeared above a spring, her image accompanied by the scent of roses. In New Jersey she showed up in the blue spruce trees in Joseph Januszkiewicz's backyard.

The Society's mission is to investigate. To keep an open mind and consider: Is a phenomenon true or false? Are those who report an event reliable? Is it mass hallucination? A desire on some individual's part to assume center stage? The Society tries to sift through hype, keep accurate records, maintain a scientific stance.

"Do you really believe all that stuff?" her sister Rosalie asked during a recent phone call.

"What stuff?" she said, immediately defensive.

"Oh, that some people can talk to the dead, clairvoyance, haunted Xerox machines. Whatever it is you investigate."

"I believe some of it. We consider each case separately."

Rosalie, the manager of an antiques mall in Boca Raton, Florida, lives there with their mother, who's in her nineties.

"Why can't you just be Jewish?" Rosalie asked. "Why this fascination with the occult? No one *knows*—really knows—how anything happened or why it happened or why it's still happening."

"I'm not giving up being Jewish."

"Can you do both? Be Jewish and believe in the occult?"

"I don't see why not. Besides, I'm interested in haunted Xerox machines."

"Right."

Opal thought of Poppy and added, "'Anyway, why not a religion with a Mother Goddess instead of a God the Father. I like the idea of a mother. Fathers favor the boys."

Rosalie changed the subject.

Opal spends fifteen minutes cleaning out the refrigerator, eats a can of sardines and three slices of crusty bread for dinner. Then she carries a basket of laundry upstairs. As a student actress (actor), she played one of the witches in *Macbeth*. They stirred a big cauldron about the size of this laundry basket and wore long blue diaphanous gowns. They weren't evil, hungry, haglike witches like the one in *Hansel and Gretel*; instead they looked prophetic, cerulean, wrapped in wind. The director saw them as mythic, as anima figures.

Carrying the basket makes her left knee hurt. The beginning of arthritis? Are there exercises she should do? Medication?

In the bedroom, she sits on the bed. When was the last time she folded clothes? Usually she doesn't bother, just fishes out of the basket what she needs. She picks up the remote control and turns on the TV, switches from channel to channel. Nothing to watch. She turns it off, tries the radio—they're playing Brahms' *Academic Festival Overture*—and begins to fold clothes. She makes lopsided piles. Eight T-shirts of Sol's, including his favorite plum-colored one—why didn't he take it with him?—six pairs of undershorts, four pairs of black socks, three pairs of tennis socks. A pair of brown corduroy pants. She stacks her clothes on the other side of the bed. T-shirts, bras, panties—suddenly in the last year turned aqua, orange, leopard-spotted—after decades of plain white or black or beige. Then in the middle, a tower of purple towels, sheets with pink and green flowers. From the bottom of the basket she hauls up (like toes of frogs) a collection of stray socks. She thinks about throwing them out, but decides against it. Now to cram these items into drawers. Before she can do it, the phone rings.

"Yo, Mama."

It's Zach.

"Long time, no see. What's new?" she asks.

"Guess who I saw today?"

Zach likes "Guess Who" games.

Opal thinks. Someone from school? Someone from work? The old neighborhood? "Mrs. E?" (Short for Mrs. Early, Zach's kindergarten teacher.)

"Nope. Adrian."

"I was about to say Adrian." Adrian, a kid from the neighborhood, owner of a wild reputation.

"Right. Anyway, his mother died."

"What?"

"She got hit by a car, a hit and run; they never caught the guy who did it."

"That's terrible. Are you sure?"

"That's what Adrian said."

"I'm sorry to hear it." An image of Adrian's mother surfaces in Opal's mind. Young-looking, thin as a teenager, eating a candy bar at eight A.M. as she waited at the bus stop with Adrian.

"Unbelievable, isn't it?" Zach says.

"It is. How's Adrian doing?"

"Trying to get his life together. It happened a month ago."

"Terrible. I hope they catch the driver."

"Yeah."

A pause and then Opal ventures, "How's your car?"

"It's got a cracked windshield. Don't know how it happened."

"Did you call your insurance company?"

"Do they take care of stuff like that?"

"Sure. It was an accident."

A beep sounds and Zach says, "Hold on a minute. I have call-waiting." And he switches to his other caller.

Opal doodles a star on the telephone message pad. Damn call-waiting. Now she'll be judged—more or less important than his other caller.

"Can I call you later?" Zach is back. "It's Roz; she's got an appointment and needs to talk to me right now." Roz is Zach's girlfriend.

"No problem. Call the insurance company."

"Okay. Oh, by the way, there's a possibility I might move to New Mexico with Roz. We've been talking about it."

"Move to New Mexico?"

"It's a thought. Listen, I gotta go. Talk to you later."

New Mexico. And if he decides to go? He's old enough to do what he wants. Live where he wants. See the country. Settle a thousand miles from home. Why not? It's his life, not hers. Hers is here, with Sol, with the Society.

After she puts the clothes away, she picks up *Borderlines* and reads for an hour. Anecdote after anecdote of the exotic and unusual: A girl who as a child listened to the mice singing in her attic and grew up to understand the language of the animals. A woman who won a car in a drawing after her husband refused to let her take their car shopping. (Her desire was so strong.) A man who witnessed a "rose-colored light" enter his home via the kitchen window fan. A captured sea monster, a hundred feet long and fifty feet in diameter, whose cut-off and pickled head was lost when the ship transporting it went down. An eccentric inventor, Andrew Crosse, who created life from inorganic matter.

Giant human molars excavated from the Number 3 Eagle Coal Mine at Bear Creek, Montana, in November 1926. Codelike radio chatter reported from Venus in 1956 by Ohio State University. A frozen fish (ten inches long) that fell out of the sky and knocked a hole in the car windshield of two illustrators who were driving to work in Alexandria, Virginia.

Believe it or not, that's her question.

Didn't Shakespeare say, *Nothing's true or false but thinking makes it so?*

And facts? But facts shift. All those Europeans who once believed the world flat. Forefathers of the modern-day "planists" who still challenge the assumptions of the "globularists" and reject the theories of Copernicus, Galileo, Newton, et al. Who, when confronted with photographs of the earth taken from space, counter by asserting the space program is a hoax and the 1969 moon landing a Hollywood simulation. Who claim seventy-five percent of the population disbelieve in that moon landing.

Eccentrics throughout the ages. A single man believed in the power of books and bought six million of them. A group believed the British descended from the ten lost tribes of Israel. Another group insisted the earth was hollow and humans lived inside it, not on its surface. Many societies disputed that Shakespeare wrote the works attributed to him and suggested instead Pembroke, Oxford, Marlowe, Bacon, Raleigh, Queen Elizabeth, Daniel Defoe, Richard Burton, etc. One Frenchman even proposed an Arab as the Swan of Avon, a poet named Sheikh Zubair.

Opal closes the book, closes her eyes, and sleeps for twenty minutes. She has a half-dream in which a wind-filled voice says, "I don't believe in fairy tales. I have too much respect for science." She looks around for the speaker, but the room's empty except for a modern painting hanging on the wall. The painting's an abstract arrangement of shapes, and it has a shiny bluish quality as if a mirror has been shattered into a million pieces.

She wakes up and rubs her eyes, which still seem to see the phosphorescence of the dream painting. Her knee aches a little and when she gets up she wobbles for a moment, as if she were on a ship and hasn't yet adjusted to the motion. A ship heading where? Strangely, she can't remember, or is it that she never possessed this information? Behind her, the wake of the ship becomes silver, as does the horizon before her. A fog blows up, but it's thin as lace and she sails through it. Her mind is still in a luminous, floating state when the phone rings.

"Is this Opal Kirschbaum?" a jaunty male voice inquires.

In an uncertain tone she says it is.

"Is your mortgage rate too high? This is John Spivak at Associated Federal. We're offering an excellent opportunity to refinance."

"What?"

"Interest rates are falling—"

"I wouldn't refinance on the basis of a phone call."

"I'd be glad to send further information in the mail."

"No. No thank you. I'm not interested."

She hangs up quickly and checks the time. 9:30 P.M. She calls the weather and gets the conditions (clearing, seventy degrees) from a meteorologist with a southern accent. Sol should be home in an hour. She hasn't written her introduction yet nor has she received any message from the tranced-out looking figure in Sol's painting. And her sense that there's a significant act for her to perform hasn't diminished.

IT STARTS TO rain as Sol catches Route 1, just south of Philadelphia. He turns on the windshield wipers and the blades arc across the glass. His elbow hurts. From moving Aunt Rachel's marble table? And his ears. There's a ringing in his ears. It's stuffy in the station wagon; he feels like a figure in his own painting, a creature stuck in an airless mayonnaise jar.

He rolls the window down and sniffs the air. Damp. Fragrant. Fields and small farms flicker beyond the rain-pounded road. Some light remains in the sky, but most cars have already turned on their headlights, which blur in the spray of raindrops. Raindrops like tiny fish. Headlights like sea-monster eyes. Not that sea monsters exist.

The tire of a passing eighteen-wheeler throws up a stone that chinks against his windshield. A moment later a web of lines crinkles the glass. "Goddamit," he says out loud. "Goddam stupid truck driver."

Once he'd said to Opal, "I wouldn't mind being a stone."

She'd lifted an eyebrow.

What he meant was if he were a stone he'd be liberated from time and need. A cow could step on him or a truck displace him and it wouldn't matter.

Stones reputedly house the spirits of the dead.

Philosophers' stones transform metals to gold.

The stone Jacob slept on brought forth his dream of the angel.

Angels as possible as sea monsters.

Insects-in-a-jar has a stone—a pebble—in the left bottom corner among some oak leaves. Scratched on it is the same message that's tacked to the wall of his studio: *Only the wisest and the stupidest cannot change.*

Gurdjieff via his father.

On the pebble the message is indecipherable.

At the reunion Lavinia Thomas (class secretary) took a Polaroid photo of him and compared it with his picture in the high school yearbook. Forty-five years ago. Then and now. Then he'd had more hair, a go-to-the-devil look. Now his face is sunken, his hair thinned, his expression vigilant—or is it only more manic?

So what else is new?

Fifty of them in the garden room of a Holiday Inn, ten minutes from the highway, and not a soul in the room he recognized. A chef in a white hat took orders for blueberry waffles, waiters circulated with flutes of champagne.

He carried his waffle—the grids reminded him of the border of a Turkish rug—to a table. Across sat a woman in a peacock-blue blouse, the same color as that bathrobe he bought Opal when she was sick. The man on his right, a former oboe player, asked if he remembered Mrs. Stern, the English teacher, whose favorite book was *The House of the Seven Gables*. He mentioned "Doc" Ashburn, the principal.

Both dead.

Sunlight sliced through the long windows, lit up a ficus in one corner, the white cyclamen centerpieces. The man on his left, with hawk-like features, spoke of his pulmonary edema; a woman in a black turban proposed a toast.

Opal mostly wore a wig. Almost five years ago.

His closest friend had been Sidney Udall, who drove his father's Chrysler and talked about becoming a geologist and finding oil under Indian reservations. His own ambition in those days was to become an archaeologist and dig up early cities. Sidney sat next to him in Art with Mr. Lippman, whose brooding owlish face seemed to hover over the classroom. Once he arranged a trip to a cemetery to take rubbings from gravestones.

Gravestones keep restless spirits underground—where they belong.

Where was Sidney? They'd lost touch.

The woman in the peacock blouse spilled her champagne. He squinted to read her name tag. Bonnie Javits. Neither name nor face rang a bell. She leaned over and read his name tag. "Sol Olevsky," she said. "You did the yearbook cover."

Somebody remembered! An abstract-looking starburst in red and white, the school colors.

"Still painting?"

"Nonstop since I've retired. What about you?"

"I inspect meat for the state of Pennsylvania. Do you sell your paintings?"

"Sometimes." This year he'd sold one painting of a man repairing the underside of a desk and another of a man inside the TV playing cat's cradle with a viewer seated on a sofa. It was a long complicated story, but just as he started to tell it, the lady in the black turban proposed another toast and the conversation never resumed.

The road curves just before the sign for Kennet Square and Chadd's Ford. The rain lets up, and Sol adjusts the wipers to an on–off cycle. His forty-fifth high school reunion. Was he chasing a lost image of himself? Shaking up his identification with an insect trapped in a jar?

Finally the sign for the Susquahanna. He touches a map on the seat beside him. His shoulders feel cramped, his elbow hurts. And maybe the ringing isn't in his ears. Maybe there's something the matter with the car.

If only he could have said to Bonnie Javits, *I'm having a museum show next month, I recently sold two canvases for $6000 each, did you see the review of my work in the Sunday* Times?

Still, he's lucky.

As is Aunt Rachel. Still living alone at age ninety-one. A two-hour drive from the reunion to her house, a duplex in a Philadelphia suburb, surrounded by juniper borders. She'd come to the door in a purple jogging suit, her thin wisps of white hair giving her a frail, deranged look. He was her only living relative. Her sister Isabel had been dead for ten years and Rose, her other sister (his mother), dead for twenty.

His father gone for more than forty years.

"The wonder boy himself." Rachel consulted her oversized wristwatch. "Five o'clock. I've been waiting all afternoon."

"The reunion started at eleven."

"Just like your mother. Always late."

He bent to kiss her. Her skin felt dry and papery. Her old-fashioned living room displayed a maroon velvet sofa, marble coffee table, and walls covered with dozens of gold-framed paintings.

Inside the apartment, the smell of furniture polish was so strong he could hardly breathe. He felt as if the rest of the world had been shut out. As if he'd fallen inside an airless mayonnaise jar. Did Aunt Rachel believe she would live forever if she refused to open her doors and windows? Did she believe that death lacked the power to enter a closed circle?

She declined his invitation to go out to dinner and prepared a meal. First came sherry in delicate green glasses and a bowl of salt-free cashews.

"No salt, no butter, no steak. The doctors say no to everything. No fun to eat anymore."

"You must be doing something right. You're looking fit."

"No fun though. You look like your mother too. Same eyes."

Dinner was split pea soup.

"No fun to grow old," she complained.

"Any thought about a retirement home?"

Rachel put down her spoon. "What I've heard about retirement homes would curl your hair." And that was all she'd say on the subject.

After dinner, Sol walked outside. The juniper bushes seemed a maze, not the simple semicircles of a few hours earlier. The moon poured down a rose-colored light, and Sol stood quietly for a few minutes before reentering his aunt's musty rooms.

"Read me the newspaper," she said. "My eyes are going."

He sat on the velvet sofa and read to her. He repaired a leak in the kitchen faucet and dragged her marble coffee table across the room. She extracted an old photograph album from a drawer and showed him a picture of herself at age twenty-eight.

"Last night I dreamed I was young again. I wore a green hat and company came to dinner. One guest was an anarchist."

The next day Sol replaced a light bulb in the hall fixture, caulked the bathtub, rehung two Japanese prints, dragged the marble table back to its original position.

"Thank you, Mr. Handyman." Aunt Rachel hovered in the background and repeated family stories. Her father drove a car until age ninety-four without glasses. Isabel attended music school on a scholarship.

For dinner, she ordered pizza with green peppers and onions.

"Once in a while it won't kill me," she said.

Now he's driving home.

A car cuts in front of him and Sol curses it.

His elbow twinges. His ears don't feel right. Maybe he's picked up a touch of something. As he approaches Baltimore, a factory looms on his right. He likes its fluorescent lights, its geometric shape, its stark outline.

He turns on the news.

The beltway snakes around the city, then he's in the tunnel, and when he emerges, the roads are nearly empty. The amber clock beams the time: 10:30. In an hour, he'll be home.

"REMEMBER ME, I'M Sol," Sol says. Only away three days, but a moment of awkwardness.

"You do look familiar." Opal kisses him.

When he checks his studio, he inquires about the blank pad next to Insects-in-a-Jar.

"I'm expecting a message. Remember Ida Lupino? She used to get phone calls from her dead father."

"I wouldn't hold my breath."

"Edison tried to invent a telephone that would connect the real world with the spirit world."

"Right."

"How's Rachel?"

"Tough old bird."

"Did you mention the retirement home?"

"Not interested."

"How was the reunion?"

"Not so hot. Everyone a stranger." Sol finds cold chicken in the refrigerator and gnaws at a wing. Opal's about to ask more about his trip and read him the two-and-a-half completed sentences of her introduction, but he asks, "Mind if I watch the news?"

"Go ahead."

He settles onto the living room sofa, clicks on the TV, and in five minutes falls asleep.

"Welcome home," she says to his crumpled form.

Even asleep, his presence reassures her. No need tonight to start the dishwasher before going to bed—as she has the last two nights—to mask strange noises.

What did Poppy say? *The average couple spends less than four minutes a day in conversation.*

Could be.

Opal observes her sleeping husband. Sol's cucumber-green shirt matches the green in the upholstery. As if a subtle harmony exists between the man and the furniture. As if the *genius loci* has reclaimed him.

An article for the *Review* on the *genius loci*?

She mutes the TV sound.

In his three days away has Sol succumbed to alien influences? Like a transplanted tree, has he thrown out new roots and pledged allegiance to a new local god? And now back home reverted to the local influence? What did Jung say? Something about American factory workers resembling American Indians because the spirit of the continent stamped one group and three hundred years later stamped another.

But why single out factory workers?

She's been told she looks Indian.

It's her cheekbones. Rosalie, who has similar cheekbones, attributes this Asian feature to Mongols who converted to Judaism in medieval times.

Genius loci makes as much sense.

In the kitchen she brews green tea. Five years ago she'd have poured cognac, but since chemo, alcohol lacks appeal. These days she wrestles with creaky knees, loss of inches, little tolerance for alcohol.

On the TV, a picture of a burning building. Opal increases the volume to hear that a passerby risked his life to pull two children to safety. "Fools rush in," he explains.

Opal turns off the TV.

Fifty years ago, Mona Friendly had been inside the Empire State Building when an airplane rammed it. She'd stumbled down twenty stories in the dark.

Opal carries her tea to the part of the sofa unoccupied by Sol's sprawled form. Her father once cancelled his ticket on an airplane that later crashed.

An article for the *Review* on those who've sidestepped disaster?

A fact that planes and trains that crash boast a greater-than-average rate of cancellation. Before the *Titanic* sailed a number of passengers dreamed of shipwreck and cancelled. One crew member deserted.

Compelled by intuition.

Intuition not granted to everyone.

Fifteen hundred drowned when the *Titanic* sank.

Adrian's mother killed by a hit-and-run driver.

She reaches for a magazine, but her mind is picking its way elsewhere. Can Abel Moore see or hear or intuit what others cannot? Can he, like an owl, spot a rodent from a great distance? Smell as acutely as a dog who sniffs out illegal drugs? Is it some animal sense he has access to? Snakes operate by heat sensors. Bees respond to polarized light. Magnetism, barometric pressure, airborne odors, all factors that animals heed.

Plants respond to the location of the sun and moon. Why not humans? Some days she believes it, other days she doesn't. Tonight she doesn't. But belief and disbelief aren't constant. They're tides that ebb and flow, as happiness and sadness ebb and flow. For doesn't each person harbor a colony of personalities that shift and bend and whisper according to circumstance?

Tonight, she fears Abel Moore's a fraud, and she's the fool who's rushed in. Not her feeling six months ago when she published Moore's article and invited him to give the annual lecture.

Which is right?

Opal reaches for her tea.

Is "right" the question?

Why disbelieve? Not only animals and plants perform beyond the ordinary. Only a small part of any mind gets used. No one's figured out how dream logic or genius works. Hypnosis. The ability to control pain. Faith healing. Photographic memory. All talents of some minds. Hasn't a case been made for meditation? Biofeedback? Some people cure themselves of fatal diseases. The doctors can't explain it.

Anything's possible.

Why not psychometry. Clairvoyance. Predictions about the future?

In 1994 scientists will develop a car that runs on tap water.

In 1993 the U.S. will enact a federal sales tax.

An article for the *Review* on faulty predictions?

"Faulty predictions," she says, trying out the phrase.

Sol stirs but doesn't awake.

Here she sits, talking to herself, a lifelong habit. In eighth grade, a classmate teased her as she walked home from school, *I saw you talking to yourself.*

I was singing, she informed her critic, which wasn't true.

Zach knows about her soliloquies.

Once he left school early and when he heard her come in, hid in the pantry, behind the bags of potatoes and onions. Later he told her, *You had a whole conversation with yourself.*

The secret life of Opal Kirschbaum. Now you know.

You're weird.

At least I don't hide in the pantry. Or leave school when I'm not supposed to.

Sol claims she talks to herself when she showers.

What does she talk to herself about?

Sol opens an eye, struggles into an upright position. "Must have conked out."

She moves closer to him. "Glad you're home."

He puts an arm around her. "Me too."

He takes a sip of her tea, but it's cold and as soon as she gets up to take the empty cup into the kitchen, he stretches out again and falls asleep.

She leaves him on the sofa and goes up to bed.

WHAT DOES OPAL talk about to herself?

She might ask herself why sometimes she feels as brittle as a pencil point. Other times as vague as fog.

She might mention to herself that she's lived in this house for six years and doesn't know the neighbors. A sign that she's disconnected? A fragment? In need of a dog. What kind of dog?

Sol knows the neighbors.

Sol refuses to get a dog.

Inside her head, a whirl of impressions, facts, and memories. What was Geneva's word? *Anfractuous. Characterized by intricate turnings or windings*. A photograph of her mind would reveal an anfractuous state. More cluttered than Sol's garage. The difference is that her mental state is fluid. The clutter comes and goes, drifts in and out. The spotlight shifts. At the moment thoughts about stones are assuming center stage, thoughts Sol might or might not be interested in. A stone suggests the unchanging self. The philosopher's stone that transforms base metals to gold can only be extracted from the self. Is it the philosopher's stone Sol would like to be? Some other kind of stone? Stones uncovered in New England practically prove the early presence of Phoenicians or Celts or Romans.

Why is she thinking about stones?

What do these speculations mean?

They're like ants in the backyard. Fascinating to watch, but there're a hundred other types of insects crawling around out there, all competing for her attention.

Her lips feel dry. Where did she store that vial of lip balm? Should she wear her purple outfit Saturday night? Is Abel Moore a fraud? Why didn't Poppy respond to her question about love? Is love between a couple no longer the issue? What was that exercise Mr. Koldaro assigned? *Pick an apple as if you're Eve in the Garden of Eden. As if you're about to do something momentous. As if it's a matter of life and death.* Isn't picking a mate something momentous?

As a student, she scribbled a list of the kings of England before taking her history exam. The act of writing down the names forced the tides of history to make sense. But usually her thought-dreams lead to dead-ends. They appear, they disappear, they're forgotten. They scatter like brushed-aside ants. The problem is how to separate the important from the trivial.

She's too wrapped up in her work. She's carved out her little world, but what is it really? A shabby office in Takoma Park. A magazine that's constantly near ruin. Earlier this evening she looked in the mirror and saw not the violet aura that Mona Friendly sees, but the beginning of a double chin. The last time she wore her black pumps she broke a heel. She'd like a scarf to wrap around her hair and the skill to tie it. She'd like to reread *The Tibetan Book of the Dead*. She'd like to own a

dictionary of slang. She'd like to know if Rachel has all her marbles.
Does Sol think one day she'll move in with them? No way she could
live with Rachel. And why did Sol buy a fish poacher he'll never use?
Why did he go to the reunion? Hoping for a scrap of information about
his father?

She'd like to forget she ever had cancer.

She'd like ... she'd like ... to be less lonely. Some days, it's as if a
great bird with bony wings beats inside her chest. She'd like Sol ...

Why is Sol so disorganized? So cautious? Why is he available for
conversation, if only for four minutes a day, but not available to touch
the true springs of her nature.

Is it that she doesn't make the true springs of her nature available?

Does she touch the true springs of his nature?

Everything Rosalie says about her is true: she's lightweight, she's re-
linquished her true life, she's forgotten her family. Instead she investi-
gates how to turn an anecdote about celebrities believing in UFOs (Sir
Eric Gairy, the prime minister of Grenada, imprinted UFOs on his
nation's stamps) into a ten-page article.

She dithers on about the *genius loci*. Which means? She's covering
up that she has no one to confide in. She lacks control of her destiny.

Poppy lent her an article that describes an "I-Control-Me" person as
one who sprinkles salt on food before tasting it, and a "They-Control-
Me" person as one who tastes first, then sprinkles salt.

She tastes first.

Which means? She's not her own person? She's too influenced by
the opinions of others?

She doesn't want excessive salt?

She tells the same story to herself over and over. In this way she
expects its layers to settle and coalesce and lead her to the story's meaning. For example, she tells and retells the story of her last visit to Florida,
to see her mother and Rosalie.

It had been last summer, a blazing hot day. Rosalie picked her up at
the airport and drove her to their condo. Lemon trees edged the patio
and bougainvillea trailed across a low fence; everything shimmered in
the heat. Opal found her mother sitting on the patio beneath a white

umbrella. Her mother was ninety-two (a year older than Rachel), wore glasses with sequinned frames, and had lost a few teeth.

"I've decided I want to be cremated," her mother said, as soon as she saw Opal.

Opal stooped to kiss her. "Nice to see you too!"

"I know some don't approve. She—" and the old woman nodded in Rosalie's direction, "doesn't approve. But I don't see the point of going to all that trouble. Buying a coffin. Making arrangements for a site. I'd like to simplify things."

Opal looked at her sister.

Rosalie shrugged. "The rabbi won't like it, but she won't be the first."

"Could we discuss this later?" Opal asked.

"Nothing to discuss. I've made up my mind."

Rosalie brought out a tray of iced tea, but the ice in their drinks melted in seconds. Opal felt as glassy-eyed as a hypnotist's subject.

In spite of the heat, her mother wore a light blue jacket, and on the way to lunch, she read the street signs out loud, demonstrating the success of two recent cataract operations. There was nothing the matter with her hearing either, but over chicken sandwiches Opal saw that the old fury had diminished.

Later Opal watched her mother huddled in bed under an embroidered coverlet. Bottles of lotions and creams spread across her dressing table and a huge abalone shell overflowed with perfume samples. Her teeth needed attention, although her hands had remained elegant. A chair in a corner of the room, its pale upholstery slightly stained, held a heap of clothes and towels. Shoes spilled from the closet.

The gentle disorder announced that here resided a woman whose forces were scattered.

So much had fallen away.

Every night she demanded coffee ice cream for dinner.

She wandered the house at three A.M., ghostlike, in a long white gown.

A few months after Opal returned to Washington, Rosalie called to say she'd hired two aides to assist with their mother who could no longer be left alone.

GENEVA WAKES AT two A.M., gripped by a feeling of alarm. In the dark, the walls seem shadowy. Non-solid. They might topple and bury her. She throws off the covers—she's sweating—and listens to her heart pounding. It's important to stay calm. To take action. Slowly she reaches for the light and in its sudden glare reads the newspaper ad she clipped earlier in the week. *Troubled by Anxiety or Panic? Symptoms may include palpitation, shortness of breath, trembling or shaking, sweating, intense fear, or out of control feelings.* The ad lists a daytime and a nighttime phone number. She's about to dial the nighttime one when she notices the fine print: *Conducting a research trial of a new medication.*

She needs help, but who wants to be a guinea pig? She drops the clipping on the floor, gets up, pulls on her old terry cloth bathrobe, and pads into the kitchen where she pours a shot of vodka. She sits at the kitchen table, willing herself to calm down, trying to divert the stream of obsessive thoughts stampeding through her mind. She imagines herself floating on water. The water's warm and soothing and it ripples around her. It lifts her. So what if she once spent an entire week without talking to anyone? So what if the last time she telephoned her brother he didn't recognize her voice? So what if two minutes ago the bedroom walls seemed ready to collapse and crush her?

These things happen.

What's important is to stay calm, not to give in to the panic. It's not a heart attack. She's not going to die. She's floating. She will not sink. The pounding in her chest, the shooting pains in her arms and stomach are symptoms. Only symptoms. The magnetic poles haven't reversed. The flood will not come.

It's a panic attack, she's had panic attacks before.

She's not as bad as her mother, who so feared thunderstorms, she buried her head under a pillow whenever one started. She spent hours every day watching weather reports on TV and often refused to leave the house because she feared getting caught in a sudden downpour.

Her mother died from an aneurysm.

Geneva shifts her long legs and adjusts her bathrobe. Her life's imperfect. She's miscalculated. She's read too many books at the expense of her love life. She's dropped too many coins in panhandlers' cups without reducing the number of the homeless.

She sips her vodka. The cottage, silent at this early morning hour, seems twice its normal size. So far the kitchen walls seem solid. And anchored.

Best to take action.

She finds her little notebook and a ballpoint.

> *Dear Mayor Barry:*
>
> *This letter is to inform you about a dangling tree limb on the southeastern corner of Fifth and Edgewood. An arborist should prune this tree before someone is seriously injured. You remember the young woman who was killed near the German Embassy by a falling branch? Let's not have a repeat of that tragic occurrence.*

She adds *Yours Truly* and signs her name.

Then she drags an old Smith Corona out of the hall closet, sets it up on the kitchen table, and bangs out her letter. She mistypes "southeastern" and has to rummage in a drawer to find the whiteout. When she lands a job, she'll buy a computer that will simplify making corrections, but the finished product doesn't look bad.

She closes her eyes. She's floating. It's important to think positively. To redirect negative thoughts.

The moon shines in the kitchen window, creating a false dawn. Her heartbeat and thoughts have slowed, but her spirit feels chilled. The moonlight itself seems chilled, a beacon from a cold sky. She refills her glass and sits, listening. Once, when her mother was checking out weather reports, they watched on TV the devastation wrought by a hurricane: trees down, homeless citizens, ruined coastal houses.

"They shouldn't allow people to build so near the sea," Geneva had commented.

"Write and tell them. Better to light a candle than to curse the darkness." As her mother spoke, she crossed out an entry on her calendar for the next day, though the path of the hurricane lay hundreds of miles to the south.

The letter Geneva wrote ignited her writing career. She followed it by dozens of others: letters to the Mayor about burned-out bulbs in street lamps or vacant lots in need of mowing. She typed letters to the newspaper concerning the inefficiency of daylight savings time or the difficulty of finding a repair shop for a 1972 turntable. She liked to write and attempted a memoir and several children's stories. She devoted herself to the essays, reports, and term papers required for graduate school.

She addresses an envelope and finds a stamp. When she buys her computer, e-mail will render this process obsolete. But she's taken action. She hasn't succumbed to her panic. The last time she suffered an attack she baked a loaf of banana bread, careful to beat the batter sunwise—clockwise—to keep in harmony with the natural—east-to-west—movement of the sun.

Take action! That's her motto.

Outside a bird cries. What information might birds exchange at this time of night? Yeats saw birds—swans, herons, hawks, eagles—as symbols of subjectivity.

If she knew how, she'd cast a spell to entice a lover.

Not that charms work.

Once more, she conjures up an image of herself floating. She's a mermaid. A naiad. A little more vodka will sustain the illusion.

Should she compose one of those personal ads? *Lonely Amazon, bookish SWF (31), late bloomer, interested in magnetic forces, enjoys ethnic dining, ISO tall, literate SWM, not deranged.*

Listen to some music?

Back in the bedroom she switches on the radio. A symphony drowns out the birds. Whose symphony? She doesn't know or care, but the sound is lavish, and Geneva climbs into bed and lets the music roll over her. The walls, thank God, remain stable. She lies on her right side to protect her heart. Her head points north, her feet south, so that the magnetic waves that flow from the North Pole to the South Pole will help her sleep.

In ten minutes, whether because of the late hour, the music, the polar magnetism, or the vodka, or some combination of these, she closes her eyes and sleep does overtake her.

SOL DECIDES TO cut the grass. He drags the lawnmower from the shed, which provokes a twinge in his elbow. Necessary to check out this elbow. Call the doctor? Too early, at eight A.M.? Not too early for Opal, who just left for the office, so why should it be too early for the doctor? First he'll cut the grass, then call. Later in the day, it's liable to rain and wet grass is harder to mow.

He tugs the starter cord on the mower, and as the motor catches, a chip of gravel flies up and lands in a flowerbed. Like a tiddly wink. If he were a piece of gravel, would he end up in a flowerbed? In a parking lot? In a weed-filled field? Would he spot effigies in companion bits of gravel? Opal's book of "natural rock portraits" has photographs of rocks that look like Richard Nixon, Mark Twain, King Arthur.

Who decided what King Arthur looked like?

In "The Desk" a man flat on his back reaches up to repair the desk's underside. It was that upside down angle of vision he wanted. "Unusual," Opal had said. Sol didn't know how to take her comment, but the painting sold to the vice-president of a hardware store who hung it in his office.

Most of his paintings don't sell.

Because he lacks awareness? His father took Gurdjieff's movement classes in New York, which supposedly increased awareness.

Sol checks his watch.

At nine A.M. he'll call the doctor.

As he guides the lawnmower back and forth in narrow channels, he notices a terrible racket. Something the matter with the machine? The lawnmower's roaring; it's never done this before. Or maybe it's not the lawnmower, maybe it's his ears. That's it. Something's the matter with his ears. That ringing sensation last night in the car. And now the lawnmower sounding like a squadron of fighter planes. He shuts off the machine and goes into the house for cotton to stuff in his ears.

He restarts the machine. The cotton helps, but the roaring, though muted, continues. How did he suddenly become so sensitive to noise? In one day? How could such an odd thing happen? An augury of something seriously wrong?

In twenty minutes, the grass cut, Sol stands in front of his house surveying his work. He checks his watch again. Still too early to call the doctor. And which doctor? Should he call his internist? Someone for his elbow? An ear, nose, and throat guy for his ears?

While waiting, he could iron the pile of napkins on top of the dryer. Opal refuses to iron, but ironing napkins is relaxing. A simple and precise task.

The zen of ironing.

Opposite of the insect-in-a-jar feeling.

While ironing—or mowing the lawn—no time to wrestle with the angel of ...

Before he can decide what kind of angel, he notices a man in the street, staring at his house. The man lifts a camera that's hanging from a strap around his neck, focuses and snaps. Then he moves to a different vantage point and snaps again. The photographer has a triangular face and reddish hair fading to grey. He's dressed in khaki pants and a dull blue jacket. When he spots Sol, he says, "Hope you don't mind me taking a few pictures."

"What?" Sol removes the cotton from his ears.

The photographer repeats his request.

"Any special reason?" It's 8:30 in the morning. Somebody casing the joint? With a camera? But there are fancier houses down the block.

"I used to live here."

Ah! A visitor to the past. "When was that?"

The man closes his eyes to calculate. "About twenty-five years ago. My daughter Emilia was born in this house."

"Twenty-five years!"

"Early seventies. I was attached to the Australian Embassy. A pharmacist lived next door." He gestures to the square colonial on the left.

"We've lived here six years."

"Two bedrooms up from the main floor and a small bedroom downstairs."

"That's it."

"We had a lot of parties." The visitor smiles, as if seeing them again.

Sol hesitates before asking, "Like to come in and look around?"

"Oh no! That might disturb the pictures in my head. But thanks."

"Walk around and see the garden?"

The man shakes his head. "If I could just take another shot or two?"

"Go ahead."

The man refocuses his camera. The sun glints in his light hair as he clicks away. "I'll send one to Emilia. She'll get a kick out of it."

"Sure you don't want to look inside?"

"Dead sure. But thanks again." And with a jaunty salute, he strides off down the street.

Sol watches the figure turn the corner, then hauls the lawnmower back to the shed. Revisiting the past. His intention at his high school reunion? His father's intention with Gurdjieff's classes? But which past? The actual one? The one he made up?

After a handful of peanuts and a slice of pound cake, Sol phones his internist who recommends an orthopedics man for his elbow and a specialist for his ears. The bone man is booked until next month, but the ear, nose, and throat man offers Sol a slot that afternoon.

He irons the napkins.

Later, he sits on the mustard-colored sofa in his studio and opens *Peterson's Field Guide to Insects*. The book is soft and dog-eared. The introduction mentions that half the living creatures on earth are insects, that several hundred thousand different kinds of insects exist. He turns to the section on wasps. He's modeled his insect creatures on the cuckoo wasp, which has a metallic green body and two pair of transparent wings. The text notes that if you disturb this wasp, it curls into a ball.

He's given the three figures in his painting the bodies of wasps and the heads of women. One head suggests his Aunt Isabel. The second head has the face of Dorothy Lamour, whom he once met at a community meeting.

The third figure is unfinished. He could call her Emilia. Born like her namesake in this house. He could give her a sharp face like her father's, but more delicate. Give her her father's reddish hair but more golden and floating.

An angel? She already has wings, two pair, delicate and transparent with a notch in the posterior ones. Emilia sounds like the name of an angel. Perhaps she could be one of those angels of … disaffection … he wrestled with earlier in the morning.

Not an angel. Angels too mass market these days.

As he paints her, he'll discover who she is.

He sits for an hour looking at his painting but doesn't pick up a brush.

For lunch, he finishes the chicken and the rest of the pound cake.

In the afternoon he arrives ten minutes early for his appointment with the ear, nose, and throat man.

"I DREAMED I WAS a witch last night," Poppy announces. "I was wearing a long cape and flying." She turns to Opal who sits across from her. "What does it mean?"

"W-i-t-c-h may mean w-h-i-c-h," Opal says. "You're worried about 'which' way you should go. You're in a quandary."

"No news there." Poppy waters the fern on her desk from a paper cup.

"Homophone," Geneva says. "Like 'gorilla,' an ape, sounds like 'guerrilla,' an underground fighter."

Poppy turns to her fellow worker. "What did you dream about last night?"

Geneva covers her mouth to mask a yawn. She's short on sleep. Last night the walls in motion, her thoughts swarming. Did she dream? She's not sure. She says, "I didn't dream. Or if I did, I don't remember."

"Everybody dreams."

"Everybody doesn't remember."

"What about you?" Poppy redirects her attention to Opal. "Do you remember what you dreamed about?"

"I do not."

Poppy arranges three pencils on her desk in a neat line.

The phone rings and Opal picks up. It's Mona Friendly, asking for suggestions for Saturday night's menu. Mona advances straight to the point. "Do you think Abel Moore's a vegetarian?"

"No idea," Opal says.

"Aren't people who study the spiritual side of life usually vegetarians? Or vegans?"

"I'm not," Opal admits. "What about noodle salad?" She signals "Help me" by widening her eyes at Poppy and Geneva.

"Three bean salad," Poppy whispers, remembering a staple from childhood. Too bad frozen salads don't exist. Food not a priority. Didn't Vic once call her a gastronomical virgin? "Tell her to look in *The Moosewood Cookbook*." A book her mother gave her, which she's yet to open.

"Ratatouille," Geneva says. "Cold or hot." Not that she's had any, but she's read about it.

Opal relays these suggestions and adds, "Can I bring something? They served a nice black bean salad at the Cosmos and Mind Conference last month. I think I could duplicate it. I could make a Salade Niçoise."

Later, when Geneva opens the mail, she holds up a newspaper clipping. "'The apparition of a face—said to resemble Eleanor Roosevelt's—in the Houston city dump is causing massive traffic jams. Cars in the vicinity experienced two hours of gridlock yesterday as thousands tried to approach the site. Those who have gotten through report that the face appears in a triangle of light and bestows a great feeling of peace and serenity.'"

"A triangle of light surrounded by a blue border," Poppy repeats thoughtfully, as if visualizing this image in her mind's eye.

"Thousands! Yesterday it was hundreds. I'll start a file," Opal says. "I wish it were closer so we could check it out."

The phone rings again. Brenda Lovejoy, Geneva's neighbor, asking for two tickets for Saturday night's lecture. One for herself and one for her nephew, Peter. Geneva slides two tickets into an envelope and marks it.

Geneva volunteers to mail the flyers that Poppy has been folding and sticking address labels on. She shoves them into a shopping bag and sets off. A block from the office, she spots George Bluestone, their upstairs neighbor.

Where's he going? He enters a small restaurant. Geneva peers at the menu posted to the left of the door. Inexpensive, deli-style offerings. If she follows him inside, what will she do with the egg salad sandwich she brought from home?

Inside, booths line one wall, and George Bluestone sits in the second one, reading a newspaper. Geneva averts her face as she sidles by, but he never looks up. She feels like a CIA agent as she slips into the booth behind his. A guerrilla fighter.

The green leatherlike upholstery is ripped but comfortable. Almost at once, a thin waitress appears and sets down a glass of water. She hands Geneva the same menu that's in the window.

Geneva scans the menu for ratatouille but settles for French onion soup, the most exotic item on the menu. While waiting for it, she adjusts her long legs under the table and fishes from her handbag the mystery novel she always carries. She holds the open book in front of her face and, thus camouflaged, stealthily peers out at the deli's few customers. At the counter, a couple takes bites from the same slice of cheesecake; at the cash register, a woman questions her bill.

The waitress brings a tray to George Bluestone's table, and Geneva notices a sandwich and a salad. What kind of sandwich? What kind of salad dressing?

Her onion soup is hot. She blows on a spoonful to cool it, then struggles with the strings of cheese.

It's not bad.

After lunch she shadows him again. The sunlight's bright and she shades her eyes with one hand. Her quarry stops to watch two workmen taking down a dead tree. One, high up in the branches and secured by a safety belt, saws off limbs which he tosses to the worker below. George Bluestone falls into conversation with the man on the ground, but Geneva's too far away to hear any exchange.

She feels a stab of impatience. Why is George Bluestone killing time? Doesn't he have appointments? A schedule? It's interesting that, like herself, he's concerned about dangerous tree limbs, but she can't hang around forever. Besides, she's too far away to eavesdrop. Nor is it comfortable, leaning against a building, switching the shopping bag filled with flyers from one hand to the other.

The flyers!

The post office is two blocks in the opposite direction. She hesitates, but George Bluestone looks as if he could talk for an hour. To hell with it.

She marches off and mails the flyers.

Back in the office she finds Opal and Poppy engaged in a discussion about early American settlers.

Poppy holds up a magazine. "According to this article, we've got it reversed. Native Americans didn't migrate from Asia. They originated here, then fanned out to Asia and other continents."

Opal rubs a fingernail. "That's the theory that the New World is really the Old World."

"That's it. They've found artifacts in the Americas one hundred thousand years old, which contradicts those who insist that ancestors of the Indians crossed the Bering Straits forty thousand years ago."

"I mailed the flyers," Geneva interjects.

"Good," Opal says.

Poppy ignores her coworker. "Thor Heyerdahl showed that South Americans colonized Easter Island."

Opal swivels in her chair. "Lots of early settler stories. Thor Heyerdahl also proved that ancient Egyptians could have navigated the Atlantic. A fifth-century Chinese monk described a place that sounds identical to the Grand Canyon."

Geneva slips behind her desk. How would they react if she told them she followed George Bluestone into a restaurant for lunch and afterwards observed him talking to a workman on the street? Would they be interested?

Opal, possible article topics on her mind, thinks out loud. "Some claim the ten lost tribes of the Jews migrated to the U.S. and became ancestors of the Indians. A stone's been dug up in Brazil with Phoenician writing on it, which could mean the Phoenicians sailed this far. The Vikings you know about. The Afrocentrists claim Africans visited America centuries before Columbus and introduced tobacco. Also there's evidence of an early Celtic presence in America."

"What do you believe?" Poppy asks Opal.

"Go on about the Celts," Geneva says.

"They've dug up Celtic heads decorated with acorns and oak leaves— Druid symbols. They've found Celtic daggers, Celtic burial chambers, Celtic stone circles. Similarities exist between the Celtic hero Cuchulain and the Mayan hero, Kukulcan."

"The Death of Cuchulain," Geneva murmurs, remembering Yeats' poem.

Poppy thumps the magazine which now lies folded open on her desk. "The article mentions similarities between Egyptian hieroglyphics and the picture writings of the Algonquins."

The discussion continues. Finally Poppy promises to duplicate the article. Once the copier is repaired.

Geneva listens. Egyptians. Algonquins. Cuchulain. Kukulcan. Homophones? Coincidences? Is any of this significant? More or less significant than the fact that George Bluestone ordered salad and a sandwich for lunch?

WHAT DOES OPAL believe?

In keeping an open mind. A Chinese monk could have visited the Grand Canyon in the fifth century. The Celts could have established a pre-Columbian settlement on the east coast. The unfinished figure in Sol's painting could one day speak to her.

Three thousand milligrams of vitamin C a day promotes healing.

Broccoli should be eaten three times a week. High quality olive oil should replace most other fats and oils. No white bread.

Some people can penetrate the barrier between the living and the dead. Ida Lupino. The mystic poet Novalis.

UFOs and aliens don't exist.

A disciplined life is better than a hedonistic one.

Breathing is paramount. When you breathe, you inhale the universe.

It's possible to live for decades with people, yet only partially know them. People, like Mayan wells, conceal both gold rings and garbage in their depths.

Her father died at too young an age.

She would have made a strong Lady Macbeth, although she liked being a witch.

Dreams restore the psychic equilibrium and always mean something.

Each person experiences the world differently, though all are surrounded by what's unknown and unknowable.

Green tea's good for you.

Acting is believing.

It doesn't matter whether an incident is true or false. What matters is your belief or disbelief in it.

Mexico, Brazil, Bolivia, Peru, the peninsula of Yucatán were probably colonies of Atlantis.

At the theater, if a man's in the next seat, he always ends up with the armrest.

Green tea is an acquired taste.

Lying for a long time in a hospital bed attached to a lot of tubes isn't a good idea. When it's time to go, it's time to go.

Each day is a gift.

To most people she's invisible. As are all fifty-nine-year-old women. The world ignores them. She could easily become a successful spy. Slip in and out of boardrooms. Cross borders. No one would notice.

Once a great flood decimated the world. Besides the biblical account, the flood story appears in the legends of Chaldea, Sumeria, Babylon, Greece, Armenia. It also shows up in the oral traditions of many American Indian tribes, among Aborigines of Australia, and in the histories of the people of southern Asia. One South American tribe attributed the flood to the angry god, Hurakan.

Disaster can happen at any time.

OPAL ADDS CUMIN to her white bean and ground turkey chili and considers possible topics for articles. One on people who can't wear wristwatches because a chemical imbalance in their systems upsets the mechanism?

One on fishermen who can "summon" fish?

An article on exotic animals that have adapted to life in big cities? Muscovy ducks, red-eared slider turtles, Egyptian geese, black-crowned night herons, marmosets, arctic foxes, and lion cubs have been spotted in New York City.

After Saturday, it's back to business.

She'd like a vacation.

She reduces the flame to simmer under the chili. In the living room, a carton of old records. LPs. Sol bought them at a thrift shop down the street from the doctor's office. They'll end up in the garage, side by side with his other crates.

She shoves the box with her foot.

Old records?

Why did he buy them?

One day they'll become valuable and he'll sell them?

They were a bargain?

He's nostalgic for his youth when LPs first appeared?

She chops scallions and tosses them into the chili.

He collects LPs because once they spoke to him. But now, technology has rendered them obsolete. Like the spirits once thought to inhabit rivers or the demons that lived in caves, they've faded, become monuments to the past.

But she doesn't want to collect monuments, she wants to be captain of her ship, an "I-Control-Me" person, rather than a "They-Control-Me" person.

She stirs the chili. *Double. Double. Toil and Trouble.* Poppy's not the only one thinking about possibilities.

On a sheet of paper she scrawls:

1) Find another job.
2) Turn the house into a bed and breakfast.
3) Try freelance editing.
4) Start a consulting business. Consulting about what? People who can't wear wristwatches?

Fifty-nine and what to show for it? Her name on the masthead of a review that hardly anyone reads. Many loyal subscribers, but so what? Every week letters arrive. Most praise or criticize articles in the magazine, a few suggest topics. That letter on mazes pointed out that for thirty-five hundred years the labyrinth's basic design has been carved into rocks, woven into blankets or baskets, laid out in colored tiles, even cut into turf.

Used the word "anfractuous."

She answers each letter. For her maze correspondent, she enclosed the publication guidelines and invited him to submit an article.

Readers also send clippings. A recent one on new viruses driven into the atmosphere by solar winds after the Shoemaker-Levy comet crashed into Jupiter. One on a man who lived his life as a horse, pulling a cart through the streets of Boston. Another on a man who studied yogi techniques until he could ride his motorcycle blindfolded.

Should she have stuck to acting? Committed herself to changing roles, instead of foundering in full-time eccentricity. Investigating the paranormal.

What was Mr. Koldaro's exercise? *Find the subtext. For example, take the phrase "Don't go." What lies beneath it? It could mean: "I command you to stay." It could mean: "Stay if you care about me." It could mean: "I warn you, you'll be sorry if you leave."*

The subtext for the phrase, "I should have stuck to acting?" My current project isn't working out. I have fallen into a rut. I have wasted my life.

What would it be like to run a bed and breakfast?

She adds to her list.

> 5) Volunteer at a theater.
> 6) Take a year off.
> 7) Write freelance articles.
> 8) Join the Peace Corps.

Dinner consists of the white bean chili, a salad, and seven grain bread.

Between bites, Sol announces, "Sinusitis is what the doctor said I have. He prescribed an antibiotic."

"What's sinusitis?"

"To do with the sinuses."

"What caused it?"

"He doesn't know. Doesn't know how long it will last either. He gave it a name. Told me it's not life-threatening. I also made an appointment with an orthopedic man for next month."

"What for?"

"My elbow."

"What's the matter with your elbow?"

"I must have reinjured it moving Rachel's marble table."

"Reinjured it?"

"Don't you remember? A few months ago I couldn't pull my shirt on. Couldn't comb my hair in the back."

She doesn't remember.

After dinner she begins to straighten her study. *Act as if you're organized and you'll become organized.* Acting is believing.

She tosses old magazines, catalogs, and mail into a green plastic trash bag that rips when she tries to lift it. Her restlessness returns. What's the matter with her? Why didn't she remember Sol's injured elbow? Should she be taking Ginkgo biloba, which is supposed to enhance memory? Is she turning into one of those middle-aged women who falls apart? It happens. First the cancer, then the loss of an inch, next it could be ten IQ points.

She's arthritic too. Those twinges in her knee. Sol and his elbow have nothing on her.

At least the cancer's in remission.

No fun to grow old.

A few days away would help. A lake in Maine …

She bumps her ripped bag of papers down the steps. The microwave's beeping. Sol reheating his coffee.

A lake in Maine.

Opal points to the bag. "At least I'm getting rid of stuff."

Sol looks up, alerted by her tone. "Good for you!"

"I can find things if I need them! Which is more than you can do!" Opal's frustration erupts. "You lost your mother's samovar! It's buried in that damn garage! You lost those wooden Indian fabric stamps I want to hang on the wall! You lost that teapot we bought for a wedding present and had to buy another one! What's the point if you can never find the things you want? You might as well toss it all!"

Sol bangs his coffee cup down. "That's exactly what I should do! Move my stuff out! Get every single thing that belongs to me out of this house! And I'll go right along with it!"

"I couldn't ask for anything better!"

"You're incredible!"

"You're the one who's incredible!"

Neither of them means it, yet in a way they do.

It's like skating on brittle ice or playing Russian roulette. Something terrible could happen. They're both energized, their usual harmony shattered. It's thrilling, their fury a reminder of selves they'd been a dozen years ago when they were more potent, more volatile, more ready to change their lives and go out and forge new ones.

Impossible now.

A garage crammed with junk or a garage neat as a pin, they're stuck with each other. Nothing will change, until a real change takes place, a change not of anyone's volition. Otherwise, they'll stay as they are.

Sol storms into his studio and Opal sinks into a chair.

A lake in Maine … she can see it. Water bordered by pine trees. In the distance a loon calls. A green canoe glides by. In the village an antique shop displays a shelf of blue bottles.

In his studio, Sol drinks his coffee and falls asleep.

An hour later, Opal checks on him. Still sprawled in sleep. The *Titanic* could be sinking and he'd keep sleeping. She picks up his coffee cup, glances at the pad by the painting for a message, but there's no message.

At ten P.M. she's reading *Borderlines* when the phone rings.

"Yo, Mama," Zach says. "Just called to tell you I'm taking off for Colorado in about an hour."

"What?"

"Spur of the moment decision. I'm going to visit Sheila."

"Run this by me again. Who's Sheila? What happened to Roz and New Mexico?"

"Things are up in the air with Roz. You remember Sheila. She used to live in my house. We're just friends."

"Where in Colorado?"

"Boulder."

"For how long?"

"Four or five days. I need a break."

"I thought you might want to come to the society's lecture on Saturday night. We're having a psychic from Florida."

"A psychic! You know me. I don't believe that stuff. I'm too bitter."

"He should be interesting."

"I'd come if I were in town. You ever drink Evian water?"

"Sometimes."

"Know what Evian is spelled backwards?"

Opal thinks.

"Naive," Zach says. "Describes those who drink it."

"Are you trying to tell me something?"

"Not me. Gotta go. Call you when I get out there."

After the phone call Opal checks on Sol again. Still dead to the world. She covers him with a blanket, carries *Borderlines* to bed and sits up reading for another hour.

POPPY AND RUSSELL drive to Arlington for Vietnamese food. Ceiling fans whir overhead and murals deco-rate the walls. One depicts running horses, another a waterfall surrounded by bamboo.

Poppy smoothes her hair. Her diamond studs and gold hoops glint in the dim restaurant light. She studies her red-and-white placemat with its pictures of Chinese zodiac animals and announces, "I'm a Boar. Noble and chivalrous. My friends will be lifelong, yet I'm prone to marital strife." She looks up.

"Not to worry." Russell reads his placemat. "Snake. Wise and intense. The Boar is my enemy."

"Uh oh."

A slim waiter appears to take their order.

Poppy slides a pair of chopsticks out of their red paper sheath and breaks them apart. "I've been reading about Anne Hutchinson. She lived in the Massachusetts Bay Colony and had to leave the church because she disputed the teachings of John Calvin."

"The Massachusetts Bay Colony," Russell repeats. He stares beyond Poppy at the waterfall. Ten years since he took American history. The Massachusetts Bay Colony? What was it? When was it? Contemporary with Plymouth Rock? Jamestown?

"She encouraged women to believe in themselves."

The waiter brings two beers and Russell gratefully reaches for his. "I don't remember Anne Hutchinson."

"They accused her of heresy and exiled her from the Colony. Eventually Indians massacred her."

Russell's eyes lock on the running horses. He's stumped. Anne Hutchinson. Dead for centuries. A name from history. He should feel sympathetic, but she's too remote. It's like being in a room where people are discussing a character in a novel he hasn't read. Hard to stay interested. Hard to admit he never reads novels.

The waiter arrives with lemon grass chicken for Russell and mixed vegetables for Poppy. Poppy maneuvers a water chestnut with her chopsticks. "What are your religious beliefs?" she asks.

The question catches Russell by surprise. He picks up his glass but doesn't drink. "I wasn't brought up in any religion," he begins. True, but not exactly relevant. His beliefs are linked to nature. To trees and plants. To the natural world. But how convey this in words? "I like the outdoors," he mumbles. Easier to talk about Anne Hutchinson.

"I like the outdoors too. One day will you teach me the names of the trees?"

"Might take more than one day."

After dinner, they drive back to Poppy's Glover Park apartment where Poppy's downstairs neighbor has been babysitting. After she leaves, Russell suggests a foot rub. Poppy demurs. Too easy for one thing to lead to another. Sex might cloud the issue of whether she should marry Russell or not. Not the time to get carried away. Instead, the time to stay calm and collected.

She suggests watching the news. Russell agrees, and they sit on the sofa, his arm flung in comradely fashion around her shoulders.

She looks at him. Thick curly red hair. Nicely shaped ears. An outdoors person. He knows the names of trees. But should she marry him? Isn't she too young?

And what about Vic?

After he leaves, she slips into Metro's bedroom to check on her sleeping child. Metro's curled on his side, sleeping as soundly as a creature in a cave.

She bends over and lightly kisses him.

He turns onto his other side and continues sleeping.

In the living room she picks up the book that describes the life of Anne Hutchinson. Now she reads about Emily Carr, the Canadian artist, who led an isolated and unappreciated life. A woman who didn't have a show until she was in her sixties. A woman who in her entire life managed only a few exhibitions. The book, Judy Chicago's *The Dinner Party*, quotes her: *How completely alone I've had to face the world, no booster, no artistic backing, no relatives interested. No bother taken by papers to advertise, just me and an empty flat and the pictures.*

Poppy closes the book.

If only she had an outstanding talent.

But she doesn't.

SOL STRETCHES. SIX A.M. but he feels wide awake. Through the windows that overlook the back garden, he watches the sky change from ivory to blue.

The slogans tacked up around his studio urge him to take the day seriously. *The ideal is within. Only the wisest and the stupidest cannot change. You can't be at the pole and the equator at the same time.* And his favorite: *A bundle of asparagus means as much as the Madonna.*

Opal's still asleep. No doubt, she's thrown off the blanket and lies half-wrapped in the sheets, her book dropped on the floor, her glasses discarded on the bedside table.

Not unusual being awake while others sleep. Feeling keyed up. As if his brain's on fire. As if his eyesight's sharp enough to see a tree's leaves a mile away. As if he's capable of thinking two things at once. Being in two places at once.

As if he can remember a detail about his father he's never remembered before.

Another plus: at this early hour he can have an early breakfast. Opal won't stir for another hour. In the kitchen he finds a tangerine and a wedge of coffeecake wrapped in tinfoil. A cup of yesterday's coffee.

He unwraps the coffeecake and eats it.

Not a product his father would have touched. His father believed in whole grain bread. No white flour. No sugar. He stored a jar of wheat germ in the pantry to sprinkle on his cereal, modeled his diet on the books of Adele Davis. He attended Gurdjieff's classes in New York and took daily one-hour walks, summer and winter. He liked to quote the Russian guru, *Even the donkey is mighty.*

Did his father identify with donkeys? Those plodding animals. But his father hadn't been plodding. He'd been a man in a hurry. He drove like a maniac—witness that trip up Mt. Washington more than fifty years ago, the car skidding around paperclip curves, he and his mother clutching their door handles for dear life.

His father had been a man in a race. A race against what? He died when Sol was sixteen. Sol peels the tangerine and section by section eats it.

When he turned thirty he started to investigate his father's life and discovered that nothing added up. His father said he'd been born in Dubrow (in the Ukraine) but no records confirmed it. He said he'd come to this country in 1911 on the *Finlandia,* but not according to the ship's passenger list. He said he'd attended Western Michigan University in 1915–16, but the college denied he'd been enrolled. He said he'd served as a corporal in the U.S. Army during World War I and fought in France. Not according to military records.

Sol realized he'd uncovered a mare's nest.

Why had his father altered the facts of his life? Was it deliberate or the result of defective memory? Did he intend to enhance his image or obscure it? Was he hurtling towards a new identity or fleeing an old one? Did he transform himself out of some dark necessity? Some casual whim?

His mother waved his questions aside. "Don't ask," she said. He persisted and she countered, "Some things it's better not to know."

Had he served time in prison? Acted as a spy? Stumbled into a scandal? Entered the country illegally? Fallen into debt? Had a business connection begun to make life difficult?

Aunt Rachel swore she knew nothing.

Isabel, his other aunt, also claimed ignorance.

Now both his mother and Isabel are dead.

A private detective failed to uncover new information. Organizations that specialized in genealogical research provided no help. Nothing was learned from those groups that focused on uncovering adoptive families.

Samuel B. Olevsky eluded them all.

Back in his studio, Sol stares at the painting on his easel. A sixteen-ounce mayonnaise jar containing three insect figures stares back at him from the canvas.

He means to finish this painting.

Once when he was fourteen and his parents were gone for the day, he dismantled a bicycle, then reassembled it before they returned home. He wanted to see if he could do it. On hearing this story, Opal raised her eyebrow in the same way she raised it when he mentioned he wouldn't mind being a stone.

Later she told him that's why she married him.

"You didn't marry me for my good looks?"

"And for your good looks," she conceded. "But I liked the idea you might surprise me someday."

He sits in front of his half-finished painting.

These damn insects. Isabel. Dorothy Lamour. What are they doing here? Why has his subconscious dictated their presence in his painting? Emilia. Who is Emilia? How can he reveal her? Let her evolve.

Those years he worked for the city while experimenting at night. The stages he explored. In one, he took paint in his mouth and spit it at the canvas. In another, he painted with his eyes closed. In still another, he stuck a moon in every painting.

He never worried about success. Even after he sold a few canvases and received a favorable review in *Art Times*, success didn't matter. Is not success incommensurate with what is wild and bohemian?

He did what he wanted to do.

Just like Aunt Isabel. Dead now, but after she became a widow at age seventy-five, she toured Europe. In two months she visited eleven countries. The next year she signed up for the same trip. And the year after that. Friends suggested she try South America or the Far East. Spend more time in one country, explore a single culture in depth. But Isabel liked the eleven-country tour. She aspired neither to deepen nor to broaden her horizons. She repeated the same trip for ten years. Her friends proclaimed her eccentric, but she ignored them. "What else have I got to do but enjoy myself?" she asked.

Sol agrees with her one hundred percent.

POPPY LEAVES THE office at two P.M., picks up Metro from day care, and takes him to Montrose Park. She settles him in the sandbox with a shovel and retreats to a nearby bench.

It's a sunny day. In the blue sky, clouds drift like stately ocean liners.

A slight breeze ripples the sun-green leaves of a nearby tree. What kind of tree?

The sunlight makes her wish she'd brought a hat. Turning from the sun, she pulls out *The Woman's Encyclopedia of Myths and Secrets. The divinity of the sun, although usually conceived of as male (Apollo, Heracles, or Samson), was worshipped in early Britain as a female. Her name was Sulis and her principal place of worship was Silbury Hill, near Avebury.*

The Goddess! She's everywhere. In the sun. In the moon. In the earth. In the seas. She's creator of the universe. Of time. The giver of birth and death. The fount of wisdom and love and justice.

She who's called a thousand names.

Eleanor Roosevelt on the tabletop is one manifestation.

Anne Hutchinson was a manifestation.

How explain that to Russell?

Or Vic?

She'd only known Vic a few months. She met him after the train wreck, the case already in the hands of the lawyers.

It was during an icestorm when she slid into the back of his van—which said *VW Construction* on the side. Accident number two. She'd been heading to her mother's house in Arlington, had just turned onto Key Bridge.

No doubt whose fault this accident was. She rammed into him. But the roads *were* icy, and all around them cars skidded and fishtailed. She didn't feel guilty. She felt their meeting was an act of nature.

Destiny at work.

From the beginning she noted that he was different from anyone she'd known before. His restlessness set him apart. Even as they exchanged insurance information, she felt him floating away from her. His medium height and stocky build didn't anchor him. He emitted a ghostlike quality. His eyes could have been ghost eyes. Their expression radiated heat and distance. They were dark and spangled with gold flecks.

A weakness invaded her as she scribbled his name on a slip of paper. She couldn't believe it. She'd had plenty of boyfriends, once dated the captain of the lacrosse team. So Victor Wells wasn't the first attractive guy she'd established eye contact with. If you could call it eye contact, since his eyes didn't focus anywhere for long. Maybe the cold weather caused his glances to keep falling away. Maybe it was drugs. Maybe she'd stunned him by the jolt to his car.

Her breath formed a puffy cloud in the icy air. Vic stamped his feet on the frozen roadway and recommended she zip up her half-opened parka. They stood there for a few minutes, expecting a police officer to materialize, but one never did.

The next day he telephoned, in need of some detail for the accident report. At the end of the conversation they agreed to have dinner. Did the suggestion come from him? From her? She can't remember.

She went to dinner, but half a year later it was over: Vic off somewhere, she didn't know where. He'd asked her to go with him, but how could she?

Soon enough, he confessed his nomadic habits—he meant to live in a hundred different cities.

"Why?" she'd asked, suspecting she didn't want to hear the answer. They were sitting in Vic's van, he'd picked her up after her class. Only a foot and a half lay between them, but she was conscious of every inch. The heater blew a warm draft on her legs, and she took off her gloves.

She'd been meeting him every day. She couldn't get enough of him. His distracted manner made her wilder for him. His elusive glances— he seemed to be looking beyond her—made her want to compel him to look at her.

She knew it couldn't last—that she'd burn out—that he'd break her heart.

"Why?" she asked again.

He turned the key in the ignition and pulled into traffic.

"Five years ago I killed someone," he said.

"Someone?"

"A three-year-old child."

"How?" Poppy stared out the window as they drove towards the city.

He told her the story. An accident. He'd been twenty-four—he was twenty-nine now—when it happened. A little girl named Lee. He hadn't been drinking or speeding or inattentive. Lee darted into the street—a quiet suburban one—and his car hit her. No warning. One minute she was alive and the next minute she wasn't. Why did she run into the street? She was three years old.

Poppy's hands felt cold and she pulled on her gloves. "What happened then?"

"Not much. The police didn't charge me. No one blamed me, not Lee's parents, not my own. An accident. I was in the wrong place at the wrong time. The skid marks showed I was going less than fifteen miles an hour."

"I'm sorry," Poppy said.

"I sat around in a daze for weeks. Why did she choose that particular moment to run into the street? Why my car? You can imagine what I thought."

"I can."

"Afterwards I wanted to get away. It didn't matter where. I joined the army."

The winter light coming through the car window was so clear and pure that for a minute Vic imagined himself driving off in it, driving all day with Poppy next to him—this girl with the serious mouth who kept taking her gloves on and off.

But he couldn't do that.

The light wouldn't last. That much he knew. The earth itself would throw up a darkness to baffle him. The earth itself was against him. Hadn't it drawn his car to a deadly encounter? And now, whenever he considered settling down, the earth objected. Settling down wasn't permitted. His crime committed him to be the wanderer, the outcast. If he stayed, a darkness would descend. A darkness that would confuse and obliterate. He could see this.

Better keep moving.

By now, he'd gotten used to it. He perfected the art of making visits. Every year he showed up at his parents' condo—in Pompano Beach, Florida—and stayed exactly two weeks.

His army years prepared him for the life he saw he must lead.

Since his discharge, he'd lived in ten cities. He never stayed longer than six months. In six months he could figure out the one-way streets, find the best tennis courts, learn the name of a Chinese restaurant that made good Peking duck. Six months was long enough to find the all-night pharmacy but not long enough to put down roots. Putting down roots was the problem; Mother Earth objected to him putting down roots.

His construction business—VW Construction—permitted his no-madic life. He'd come into a new area, leaflet three or four neighbor-hoods, pick up enough work to last a few months. He performed every kind of small job: he painted, installed skylights, remodeled rec rooms, retiled kitchen floors, repaired broken windows. A gypsy handyman, but expert, whose careful work habits impressed his customers, who invariably recommended him to their friends. Sometimes Vic thought about settling down and expanding his business. But as soon as the idea sprouted, he uprooted it.

Nothing permanent.

What he hadn't counted on was meeting Poppy.

She removed her gloves—again!—and twisted a ring, a dark red gar-net, and for no reason Vic saw that if he weren't careful, he could fall in love.

He turned his attention to the road. They were driving down Route 1, in a steady stream of slow-moving traffic, and absentmindedly he read the signs in the strip malls adjacent to the highway: *Hunan Ham-let, Petco, Arcadia Music*.

He glanced at Poppy as she stared out the window in the pure winter light. A thin girl inside a bulky parka. No hat. Her fair hair pulled back, two pairs of earrings, a surprisingly serious mouth. Nervous too. She hunched against her door, bit her lip.

He was surprised he'd told her about Lee, but somehow it slipped out. She'd listened seriously, then told him that on her way home from a weekend away, her train derailed and a number of people were killed. That she'd been lucky to get out alive.

They continued seeing each other. He gave her his elephant-hair bracelet. She presented him with cuff links. Every day he picked her up. They talked. They ate dinner together. They slept together. The electricity between them didn't seem to be decreasing.

In fact, just the opposite.

That was one of the reasons he came up with a variation on his usual plan; she could come with him! They could get married if she wanted—he astonished himself—he, Victor Wells—proposing marriage!—or not—whatever she wanted. And why not? He was doomed to wander. No spot of earth would remain hospitable to him for more than a few months, but that didn't mean someone couldn't accompany him.

Poppy thought about it—a part of her wanted to go—but in the end she refused. What kind of a life would it be, to be a rolling stone?

Why couldn't he stay?

Nothing terrible would happen.

Two months after he left, she discovered herself pregnant.

She looks at two-year-old Metro patiently scooping sand. Metro inherited Vic's gold-flecked eyes, but father and son are strangers to each other and likely to remain that way.

SOL LOOKS UP "sinusitis" in *The Columbia University College of Physicians and Surgeons Home Medical Guide*. *A complication of a cold or other viral infection of the nose and throat.* He turns the page. *Using decongestant nose drops and inhaling steam may be helpful in many cases.*

Not a word about the ringing in his ears.

Why had he forgotten to mention the ringing in his ears to the doctor? That was the reason he made the appointment. How could he have forgotten to mention it? An oversight. But it could be significant. Maybe he's been misdiagnosed and doesn't have "sinusitis" at all. What's that other condition? "Tinnitus?" Maybe that's what he's got. He looks the word up in his guide. *A ringing or buzzing in the ears or inside the head …. In the most severe cases tinnitus even interrupts sleep.*

That sounds more like it, though he hasn't lost any sleep.

Also—he listens for a moment—the ringing seems to have stopped. A relief.

Not easy getting old. Always something. Impossible to predict what next.

Randomness rules.

Like those games he once played. Sprinkling sand on a glue-smeared canvas and letting chance determine the design. Juxtaposing random fragments. If you keep at it long enough, the real world starts to shift. Objects dissolve into other objects. The insubstantial becomes solid. The impenetrable turns to air.

It's what you train yourself to see. A thing is what you believe it to be. An egg can be the size of an elephant. A shadow can be an ingredient in a salad. Does Zach know this? Where did Opal say he was off to? Colorado? Flying around the country. He'd better be careful or he'll fly too near the sun and take a tumble. But Zach likes the risk. He likes the thin atmosphere up there, the coldness. Maybe he fools himself into thinking the sun itself is cold.

Only superficial resemblances between himself and Zach. Zach's inherited his eyes but developed his own obsessions. He doesn't identify with a trapped insect. He's not stuck. He doesn't brood about the past. He's free and flying in the vicinity of the sun. He's not bothered by "sinusitis" or "tinnitus" or whatever it is.

Except in emergencies, he neglects to consult a doctor. A few cooking accidents. When he sliced his hand chopping tomatoes and required six stitches. When he almost severed a thumb. Otherwise he assumes he'll get better. He always has. The headaches he complained of—while refusing to visit the ophthalmologist—disappeared after a few months. The eardrum he punctured while cleaning it with a cotton swab healed on its own.

He sees his dentist twice a year.

Which proves?

Nothing proves anything. Context is all. An unusual context reinvents the world. Consider a human skull attached to a bird's body. Consider a coffeepot full of ink. Consider the pages of a book fabricated from wool.

Everyone's striving. Advancing a point of view. Hoping to be noticed. Hoping to emerge from the crowd. Hoping to produce an artifact
of note or rarity. That guy out west who sewed old buttons on every
inch of his clothes, his boots, his hat, even tacked them onto his guitar.
Called himself the Button King. Eccentric, but people paid attention.
The guy who planted grass seed all over his dirt-packed car and wa-
tered it until grass sprouted. Then he drove around town in a vehicle
that looked like a giant chia pet.

The urge to be noticed.

The urge to build. To discover what they can do. If they can do it.

The stubborn insistence on listening to one's inner voice.

How can he be expected to listen to his inner voice when there's
that ringing in his ears?

He reshelves the medical guides and decides to wash the breakfast
dishes.

The hot water feels good. The lack of hot water in early communi-
ties was a major drawback. The Romans constructed hot baths, but
after the Romans, bathing suffered a decline. Americans have plenty of
hot water but suffer from impersonality. Too many unknown neighbors, unknown coworkers, unknown relatives. In Rachel's box of family photos, most of the faces were unfamiliar.

Sol holds a plate, then a glass under the stream of hot water before
fitting them into the dishwasher. Opal doesn't always rinse dishes as
carefully as she should. She assumes the dishwasher will do it all, which
it won't. They need a thorough rinsing first. He reaches for another
plate, but drops it. Damn! It shatters into six or eight pieces. One of the
blue-rimmed breakfast plates and there aren't that many left. Carefully,
he extracts the pieces from the sink and spreads them on the counter,
spends a minute matching up the pieces, but what's the point? He could
glue them together, but it's hard to do an exact job. And the plate's not
valuable.

He ends up dumping them in the garbage container under the sink.
Broken pieces like all those unknown family members. Each piece a
part of the puzzle, but the whole not retrievable. The whole's like

Humpty Dumpty. Maybe someone could reassemble the entire picture, but not him. An experienced archaeologist can take one shard and from it derive the complete water pitcher. Envision the life led by the culture that used it. A paleontologist can reconstruct a brontosaurus from one bone. Figure out the savannahs the dinosaur roamed in, the ferns he nibbled. But out of context they make little sense.

Of course, in an unusual enough context, they might assume a new life. A collage of broken pottery shards? It could fly. On his knees, he roots around in the garbage to retrieve the pieces of broken plate. Why didn't he think of making a collage before he tossed the pieces? Never mind, he's got most of them now. In a drawer he finds a paper bag and dumps the pieces inside. Now the puzzle's back in the box. Part of the puzzle. Easy enough to collect more material. Pick up cheap but interesting plates at flea markets and smash them. Maybe add broken flowerpot pieces.

For the moment he'll store the start of his collection in the garage.

I HAD... PROPOSED for our consideration that whatever the great poets had affirmed in their finest moments was the nearest we could come to an authoritative religion, and that their mythology, their spirits of water and wind were but literal truth.

Yeats in the 1880s.

Geneva sits up in bed rereading her dissertation, which contains this quote from Yeats' *Autobiographies*. Always a pleasure to reread the great poet. Man on a spiritual quest. Yeats joined the Dublin Hermetic Society, investigated Theosophy, Gnosticism, Cabalism. He studied *the wonders of Eastern philosophy*, reincarnation, the belief that man can achieve perfectibility, that he asserts himself by touching his higher self.

Poppy would say woman touching *her* higher self.

It's one A.M. Friday morning. To prevent another sleepless night, Geneva's hauled out her dissertation. Reading it usually sends her off in ten minutes.

About Cabalism, she's written: *The doctrines of this group subscribe to a Supreme Being or En Soph (Endless or Boundless) who is supposed to have created the world indirectly by the process of a series of ten emanations (Sephiroth or Intelligences) of diminishing strength. This lessening potency accounts for the imperfection of this world and the reason for the "creation" was the desire of the En Soph to be active and to be comprehended.*

Geneva reads these sentences twice. Did she actually write them? What do they mean? Ten emanations. She knows what "ten" means. She knows what "emanations" means. *Coming out from a source; radiations.* Ten emanations. Who dreams such stuff up? When she wrote these sentences, she understood them, but now ... she's not sure. After three months volunteering at the Society, she's not sure of much. What does a vision of Eleanor Roosevelt have to do with "man's [or woman's] fall from and return to the perfectibility of light?" What do Blob stories have to do with the journey of a soul?

Maybe she should put her dissertation away and resume her detective story.

She's about to do this when she hears something. Unusual on her quiet street. What is it? She snaps shut the bound black volume of her thesis and sits listening.

Music.

At this hour?

She climbs out of bed and discovers the music's louder in the living room. She opens the front door and the music's louder still. Someone's turned his music up full volume at one A.M.! Blaring, pulsating music. Her cottage is practically vibrating.

Someone driving by, with a car radio blasting full force? But there's no car. Pulling her terry cloth robe tighter around her, she cautiously descends her front steps and looks around.

Next door is the source of the noise. Brenda Lovejoy's house. No doubt about it. Every light ablaze. Geneva hesitates. She's lived next door to Brenda for four years without incident. What's going on? Should she stroll over and ask? Telephone?

Six rings before the phone's picked up and a male voice informs her Brenda's working the night shift.

"Who are you?" Geneva asks politely. "I live next door."

"Peter. I'm Brenda's nephew," the voice says.

"I wonder if you could turn your music down a little."

"Sure, didn't mean to disturb you."

Geneva thanks him and hangs up. At the kitchen table she waits for the music to fade. It doesn't. Instead, it gets louder. She sits there for fifteen minutes and the music continues. She calls again.

"Sorry," Peter says. "I got distracted. I'll turn it down right away."

"I'd appreciate it."

The volume doesn't decrease. Geneva waits for ten minutes. Then she dials 911.

"Care to give your name?" the officer who takes her call asks. Geneva thinks twice, then gives it. The police car arrives promptly, but though she stands in the dark and peers out her living room window, she can't see a thing.

This time the music does subside.

Geneva returns to the bedroom, picks up her dissertation, then lays it aside. Her mind refuses to focus on Yeats' quest to merge finite and infinite. Nor does her detective novel hold her attention.

Why would Brenda's nephew say he'd turn his music down but not do it? Why would he be playing loud music at this hour?

Drugs?

Maybe his behavior's typical. Maybe she's out of touch.

She's led such a solitary life these last six years. She's read dozens of books and written a dissertation. She's investigated Yeats' spiritual quest, but never considered the spiritual quest of someone like Peter.

When she falls asleep she has a curious dream. She's in her kitchen and opens the refrigerator. Inside she sees a large frozen fish. She stares at it for a moment, then closes the refrigerator. A feeling of sadness overtakes her. This feeling's still with her when she awakes the next morning. She lies there, remembering her dream, not wanting to forget it.

When she sees Opal, she'll ask what it means.

DRIVING TO THE office on Friday morning, Opal passes the school where she and Sol argued about the coffee-pot. They'd stopped for the school's annual yard sale. A canvas awning sheltered tables covered with books, children's games, household items. Opal browsed the books, but even when a woman with green eyelids announced that all paperbacks were now half price, she found nothing.

At the household items table she examined a cheese board. She was eyeing a mixmaster when Sol came up.

"Need one of those?" He poked the mixmaster. "Everything's half price now. You can probably get anything on this table for five dollars."

"No place to put it."

She strolled until she saw an espresso machine.

"Look," she said to Sol.

She'd always wanted an espresso maker.

"How much?" Sol called to the woman with green eyelids who was standing by the books. He pointed at the coffee maker and the woman came over.

"I can let you have it for twelve dollars."

"Twelve dollars!" Sol said.

"Is it all here?" Opal asked.

"I think so. These are mucho dinero in the stores."

"A brand new one's not that expensive," Sol scoffed.

"I could let you have it for ten," the woman conceded.

"Nope," Sol said. "We don't even know if it works."

"Are there directions?" Opal asked.

"No. But they all work the same," the woman said.

"Come on," Sol said. "You don't want this. You don't even know if it's all here. Or if it works."

Opal unscrewed the top and looked inside.

Sol watched impatiently.

"The carafe goes with it, right?" she asked the woman.

"Of course it goes with it," Sol said. "Come on."

Opal walked away with him, but she was irritated.

By the time she got to their car, a block away, she was steaming. She got in and as soon as Sol slid behind the wheel she said in a tight angry voice, "You never gave me a chance to decide if I wanted it or not!"

"For god's sake!"

"Right. Act disgusted! But why is it you have to decide everything?" Her voice rose. "I cannot stand to shop with you!"

Sol gripped the steering wheel. "Here we go again! The original Miss Shrinking Violet! For the first time in your goddamn life! You didn't buy that machine because I didn't want you to! Don't make me laugh!"

"You never gave me a chance to figure out if I wanted it or not!"

"Nothing on that table should have been more than five bucks! Everything was supposed to be half price! That woman just picked a price out of thin air!"

"It was a good buy!"

"If it works!"

They were sitting in the car, both furious.

Opal hissed, "You buy record players that don't work! Battery testers that don't work! Why is it okay for you to buy things that don't work but not me?"

"This is ridiculous! Why are you always giving me a lecture? First, it's my fault you didn't buy the machine, and now I get a lecture! When do I lecture you?" Sol's face had turned red.

"You intimidated me!"

"I intimidated you! That's the joke of the century!"

"It's true! You did. I stopped to look at it and immediately you decided it was worthless junk."

"Good god!"

A moment of silence.

Opal fastened her seatbelt.

More silence.

Finally Sol started the car.

They drove about a block.

"What do you want to do now?" Sol asked in a strangled voice.

Opal shrugged.

"Do you want to go home?"

"I'm thirsty."

Sol stopped at a convenience store, went in, and returned with a Diet Coke.

He handed it to her and said, "Look, if you really want that machine, you can go back and get it."

"I don't know if I want it or not. I never had a chance to decide."

"I'll drive you back. I won't go in." He reached for his wallet and extracted a twenty-dollar bill.

"I have money," Opal said stiffly.

"I'll drive you back."

"I don't know if I want it."

Sol returned to the school.

At the table Opal said to the woman with the green eyelids, "I was looking at this machine a few minutes ago with my husband. Would you take less than ten for it?"

The woman tugged at her skirt. "I could let it go for eight."

"Do you know how it works?"

"Not exactly. But they're available in department stores. Someone there could probably help you."

Opal unscrewed the top and looked inside again as if she might find instructions etched on the coils. But there was nothing there. The machine looked almost new.

"You're sure everything's here?"

"If not, bring it back next year and donate it for a tax deduction."

Opal pointed to a nozzle on the side. "What's this?"

"It froths the milk for capuccino."

Opal paid the eight dollars and watched the woman wrap the machine in tissue paper and pack it in a recyclable string bag.

Back in the car she said to Sol, "I got it for eight."

"Three dollars too much."

They stopped at a supermarket for a pound of espresso roast.

At home, she unwrapped the machine and set it on the kitchen counter.

It was handsome, with a good-sized glass carafe.

Sol washed it inside and out.

"I wish we had the instructions," he said.

"We'll figure it out."

Opal made a carafe of coffee, but it turned out thin and weak. When she tried to froth the milk, it splattered all over.

Sol rummaged in the garage and unearthed an article on espresso makers in an old *Consumers Report*. No rating for their brand, but after reading the article Sol began talking about steam machines, pump machines, and stove top models. On their way to dinner, he suggested they stop at a discount store to look for a similar machine in an open box so they could check out its instruction booklet.

They didn't find an open box.

The next day he suggested they scout the department stores at the mall. Opal found a booklet for a similar machine which described how to froth milk and pointed out that weak coffee meant the grind wasn't fine enough.

Sol spent thirteen dollars on a book telling how to make espresso.

At home, Opal ground the beans for a full minute.

This time the coffee turned out thick and strong, and a thin layer of foam appeared on top.

"Crema!" Sol shouted, who'd been reading the book. "Not bad! Eight dollars for a machine that makes crema!"

ZERO HOUR. ABEL Moore comes tomorrow. At the office, Opal reaches for the fall issue of the *Zoetic Review* and reads "Psychometry and Joshua Quinn" straight through. Then she rereads it. How he found money lost for forty years. Six thousand dollars. Found it inside a candy box.

Now to finish her introduction. The office is quiet. No distractions. No excuses. She sharpens three pencils, rereads the two-and-a-half sentences she wrote six days ago. Waits for a third to suggest itself. Thank god, it does. *Abel Moore has addressed audiences at the American Psychological Association and the International Association of Paranormal Researchers.* That's good! Makes him sound credible. The American

Psychological Association doesn't ask just anyone to speak. *He's received grants from the Le Mars Group, a Scientific Foundation, to facilitate studies of known forms of energy utilized in non-standard ways (for example, radio waves used to cook a steak).* Now she's into it, the sentences rolling like marbles. *In June he'll conduct a workshop at a five-day "psychic" retreat at the Asilomar Conference Center in Monterey, California.* She's starting to list topics to be covered at the retreat—psychic surgery, psychic archaeology, psychic criminology—when Poppy arrives.

Opal signals silence with a raised finger to her lips.

Poppy takes the hint, slides noiselessly behind her desk.

Opal writes, crosses out, writes some more, mutters, "A workshop on pendulums and one on retrocognition."

"Retrocognition?"

"Directly sensing the past."

"Ah." Poppy jots the word down on a yellow pad. She'd like to ask more but doesn't dare. Retrocognition. A phenomenon she's never heard of. One of a million phenomena she's never heard of. Directly sensing the past. In the past, the Goddess reigned supreme. Possible to experience that? Could someone skilled in retrocognition directly experience a Goddess-run society?

Opal writes on. When she adds the final period, she looks up and rubs her eyes as if emerging from deep water. "Can I run this by you? It's supposed to take three minutes."

"I'll time you." Poppy reins in her straying thoughts and focuses on her wristwatch.

At this moment, Geneva hurtles into the room. Her uncombed hair and untied laces in her boots signal a problem.

Bag lady, flits through Poppy's mind.

"What's up?" Opal asks.

Geneva drops her African-style, striped straw handbag on her desk. Then she reaches into the bag and draws forth a rock. An ordinary-looking rock, about the size of a fist. She raises it aloft as if displaying a championship trophy.

"Rock," Poppy says. Why does Geneva always make her feel like she's in the second grade?

Geneva hands her the rock. "This was thrown through my window in the middle of the night." Her tone is so neutral she might be announcing that she ate sliced bananas on her cereal that morning.

"What?" Opal barks. "Let me see that."

Poppy obliges.

Opal turns the rock over and over as if somewhere on its surface a clue might exist as to its recent travels.

"I found it on my living room floor this morning. Surrounded by broken glass." Geneva straightens her shoulders. The winds of adversity will not knock her down. Someone hurled a rock through her window. It's terrible. It's insane. But ... it's also exciting. A small segment of her brain is jumping up and down in elation. Something's finally happened to her!

She drapes her jacket over the back of her chair and tells them about Peter's late night music, her calls to him requesting him to turn it down, her call to the police.

"Strange," Poppy says.

Opal puts the rock on Geneva's desk. "Did you call the police this morning? When you found the rock?"

Geneva bends to tie a shoelace. "I will. After I talk to Brenda. She works the night shift and sleeps in."

"I wouldn't wait," Opal advises.

"I'm not sure he's the one who threw it."

"Are there other lunatics in your life?" Poppy asks.

"No," Geneva admits. Not much in her life except a stack of poetry books.

"There're crackpots out there," Poppy goes on. "That guy in Boston who stalked his ex-girlfriend and killed her."

"This guy's not my ex-boyfriend."

"He's not acting normal," Opal says.

"You didn't hear the glass breaking?" Poppy asks.

"I slept like a log. I dreamed I found a frozen fish in the refrigerator."

"A frozen fish?" Opal says.

"A whole one. It was speckled and so big it took up an entire shelf."

"A cold fish," Opal says, thoughtfully.

"I'm a cold fish?" Geneva asks. Maybe she is. Maybe that's her problem. She's been so wrapped up in her studies.

"Fish symbolize the spiritual life," Opal says. "You're concerned about the state of your spiritual life. Feel it's in cold storage."

"I'm not sure I have a spiritual life," Geneva says.

"That's what's worrying you."

"Call the police," Poppy says.

Geneva promises she will as soon as she talks to Brenda.

IN THE AFTERNOON, Sol scouts the neighborhood. What's new out there? When he worked downtown, he checked out the city during his lunch hour. Noted new buildings and boarded-up old ones. The urban landscape.

A pity Opal didn't invite John West of the Early Sites Society instead of Abel Moore. He'd like to hear John West discuss that pre-Columbian village unearthed in New England. A village with standing stones, megaliths, fireplaces, drains to prevent flooding.

New deck going up on the corner house. Almost complete. The house dissimilar to its neighbor, inappropriate for an ancient village where they built every house the same. Who owns this place? Grey-haired gentleman with a bulldog. No name comes to mind. Not like in ancient villages where people knew each other.

Had to know each other.

Now life proceeds among strangers. Everyone a John Doe.

At the neighborhood park, Sol examines the stand of holly trees planted by the local landscaping committee. Near the trees, he spots a discarded candy bar wrapper.

Could Abel Moore figure out who dropped it? The grey-haired gentleman with the bulldog? A stranger from a foreign country who'd already forgotten both when and where he was born? Would the inhabitant of an ancient village pick up the candy wrapper? Or its prehistoric equivalent?

He picks it up.

THAT NIGHT GENEVA sits at her kitchen table skimming an anthology of Yeats' poetry. She stops at:

I must arise and go now
And go to Inisfree.

Inisfree. But it's not the simple life she wants. She wants a town with a university. A university with a vacancy in its English department. Maybe out west. Or in Alaska where men outnumber women ten to one.

The years she's wasted. Semester after conscientious semester. Never turning a paper in late. Never missing a class.

Sitting through Moore's lecture won't be a problem—she's expert at sitting through lectures—but Mona's dinner before is sure to be a nightmare. What should she wear? The green silk? The navy suit she bought for interviews? Maybe she'll come down with the flu and be too sick to go. But if she's not too sick, what will she talk about? Poetry? *The fascination of what's difficult / Has dried the sap out of my veins....* Will anyone want to discuss Yeats' lines? If only she were skilled at drawing other people out. But she's not. Because she's a cold fish? Out of touch? Shy? Surely topics exist she can discuss with the Society's board members. But which ones? Yeats' cyclical theory of history ... though her understanding of it is flawed? The twenty-eight phases of the moon? Her campaign against dangerous tree branches? Her conviction that sleeping on a north–south axis promotes good luck? Helps keep the walls stable. Or she might mention that a neighbor's nephew recently hurled a rock through her living room window in the middle of the night.

POPPY HUNCHES IN bed over a book that contains thumbnail sketches of forgotten women. Almost forgotten. She reads about Mary Dyer, a seventeenth-century Quaker, who was forbidden to preach and eventually was hanged.

She reads about Sophia Haydn, who graduated with a degree in architecture from MIT in the 1890s. At age twenty-two she won an award to build the Women's Building at the Columbian Exposition in Chicago in 1893. Her work was harshly criticized as "women's work." She never built another building.

She reads about Carlotta Ferrari, a nineteenth-century Italian composer who was arrested and forced to stand trial for the crime of being a female composer.

IN HER STUDY, Opal boots up her computer and clicks to go on-line. Under her screen name (OpalK) she types in her password and listens to the modem squawk as it dials in. After a few screens pass and she's welcomed into the system, she clicks the mailbox icon. Three pornographic solicitations appear. Victoria 63 advertises *Ladies Who Know How To Say Goodnight In A Special Way*. Forbidden Passion promises the *Ultimate In Female Erotica*. *Our Live Sex Shows Will Make Your Computer Screen Sizzle.* Casey 631 boasts *Big things come in small packages. Beautiful male models!*

Why me, Opal wonders, as she deletes the messages. Don't people have better things to do?

Such as researching article topics for the *Zoetic Review*. What she has in mind is an article on the enneagram. The enneagram (a circle divided into nine equal parts) produces a triangle and an uneven six-sided figure when the points are connected.

She clicks the Internet icon, types in the address of the *Skeptic's Dictionary*, waits for the page to come up.

A relief when it does. She's a novice Web user and half the time some malfunction prevents her from going where she wants to go. Why can't she be one of those people who's able to find the answer to any question on the Web within ten minutes?

The enneagram. A circle divided into nine parts. A mandala. Related to the maze, also a mandala. The web site states that the enneagram, *a symbol which Gurdjieff derived from the Kabbalah's tree of life, shows the whole universe, the laws of three and seven, and how people cross the inter-vals of development via shocks administered by a Man Who Knows.*

Why the laws of three and seven, not the laws of three and six?

Is "Kabbalah" spelled with a *K*? She's sure she's seen it with a *C*. And with one *b* and without the *h* on the end. Cabala. Cabalist. She'll have to look it up.

Article material?

An article Sol might appreciate?

She seeks further information. Perspective. A sense of balance. For this, the *Skeptic's Dictionary* is excellent. The entry under enneagram covers several pages and calls the figure *a mystical gateway to profundity beyond your wildest dreams. Entire metaphysical systems, psychologies, reli-gions, cosmologies … are to be found by looking into the enneagram.* Tongue in cheek, but useful. She skims the account and learns that this symbol has been co-opted by New Age practitioners. No surprise there. One paragraph discusses the nine personality types based on the nine points of the enneagram. The nine types are the perfectionist, the giver, the performer, the romantic, the observer, the trooper, the epicure, the boss, the mediator.

She clicks to take the "Quick What Type Are You Personality Test," but receives instead the message: *499 Server Throttled Temporarily. We are sorry. Due to a high number of requests for the URL, it has been made temporarily unavailable. It will become accessible again within the hour.*

Does this mean there are scores of people out there wanting to take the same personality test she wants to take? A personality test based on the enneagram? At one A.M.?

Nine types of personality. She'd be?

The observer.

She clicks on Gurdjieff and scrolls through an unflattering biographi-cal sketch of the Russian guru who, it turns out, was born of Greek and Armenian parents. One quote attributed to him reads: *If all men were to become too intelligent, they would not want to be eaten by the moon.*

Which means?

A saying Sol might tack up in his study?

She clicks to take the test again. But the site remains off-limits. Nine types of personality. How might these types relate to the I-Control-Me/They-Control-Me personality assessment?

She prints out the available material on the enneagram, then signs off. Her computer reports she's spent twenty-seven minutes on-line.

Nine points of the enneagram. Nine points of connection. She studies the printout of the nine-sided drawing that accompanies the text. An odd-looking launching pad for meditation. A rose window so transparent that the winds of freedom seem to be blowing right through it.

The ringing phone derails her train of thought.

It's Zach.

"How's Colorado?" Opal asks.

"I spent the last three days in California."

"California!"

"I visited Cindy; she lives in Long Beach."

"Cindy? What happened to Sheila?"

"Sheila had a change of plans. You remember Cindy. She used to live in my house."

"I'm not sure I remember Cindy."

"Spur-of-the-moment decision. I flew to Colorado, then caught another plane to California."

"For three days?"

"It was great!"

"Must be nice to be rich."

"Yeah."

"Where are you staying?"

"In Boulder. With friends. One thing, I lost my wallet at the airport."

"What?"

"I put it down on the hood of the rental car and forgot it."

"Did you go back and look around?"

"Yeah. And I asked a few people."

"Do you need me to wire you money?"

"Nope. I called in case someone calls you. I'm not going to worry."

"How much money did you lose?"

"Four hundred dollars in travelers checks."

"Call and report it. You can get that money back."

"I already called."

"How about credit cards? Did you report them."

"Not yet. I've only got one, but no one can use it. It's maxed out."

"You still have to report it. Sure I can't send money?"

"Thanks but no thanks."

After the call, Opal treks downstairs to check the message pad next to Sol's painting. No message. Sol's stretched out asleep on the sofa. Night five. She collects the sections of his fallen and scattered newspaper and folds them.

In bed, she picks up *Borderlines* where she reads that in 1987 five of the world's six best milers all had given names beginning with S. Steve Cram, Steve Scot, Steve Ovett, Said Aouita, and Sebastian Coe.

Synchronicity.

She reads about a Florida woman who received telephone calls from a dozen dead presidents. She claimed they left their numbers, also the date and time of their calls, on her caller ID box.

Not likely. Still, anything's possible. Perhaps, under certain circumstances, the Florida air thins enough to let such messages through.

A message on a caller ID box.

It could happen.

Maybe she should get caller ID.

Part Two

YOU REMIND ME of a Man.

What Man?

Man of Power.

What Power?

Power of Hoodoo.

Hoodoo?

You Do.

Do What?

Remind Me of a Man.

What Man?

The kids' round replays in Abel Moore's head as he attacks his airline lunch. Cheese and crackers, broiled chicken, green salad, hard roll, butter pat, tiny cup of salad dressing, tiny cream puff, coffee. All neatly set in the compartments of a plastic tray like a box of watercolors. Man of Power. That's what they call him. Man of Hoodoo.

He adjusts his seat belt. A big man, the kind airplane seats aren't designed for, he overflows a little into the empty adjacent seat—thank god it's empty—and stares out the window. Mounds of thin clouds in the blue sky. He's in seat 28A. Twenty-eight. A mystic number. Twenty-eight days in the lunar cycle. The multiple of four and seven. Four points of the square. The abacus table that became the child's hopscotch game. The chessboard, a work table for intellectual initiation. And seven. Seven days of the week. Seven vibrations of light—the colors of the rainbow.

He chews a cracker, brushes away the crumbs, stares at the clouds. Possible to dissolve them? White Elk was a "cloud buster." Brought rain by speaking with sky spirits that he met on magical flights.

A man who kept his eye on the ball.

A man who was lucky.

Abel Moore struggles to cut the chicken, his back rigid against the high seat, his wide, creased face anxious and intent, his eyes heavy-lidded, his grey-streaked hair disheveled and weedlike.

Not a spiritual-looking face.

And, until five years ago, not a spiritual man.

Instead, a businessman. Owner of an auto-glass store in Jacksonville, Florida, which he had to sell during one of those recessions. Six months later Helen died. Diagnosed with lung cancer in February and dead by April. In one year wife and business gone. His daughter, Deb, grown up and established elsewhere, a lawyer for a public action group in Seattle.

Sixty years old and back to square one.

But trouble comes in threes, and he'd only suffered two disasters, so he wasn't too surprised when number three showed up. Number three was the tumor. A series of headaches alerted his doctor. A tumor on the brain. The doctor predicted it would be benign, which it was, but it had to be removed. The surgery took seven hours, the recovery almost seven months.

Unanchored, melancholy months.

The loss of his wife, of his business, of his health.

But he recovered. And thought: What more can happen? The answer came the night of Marianna Reed's party. Helen's old friend invited him and several others for the evening, and someone suggested it might be fun to contact the dead via a Ouija board. A little macabre, he thought, but agreed. Marianna rummaged through her shelves until she found the game. The planchette was missing, so she substituted a whisky glass. There were six people there, and they took turns. Two at a time, fingertips on the glass, eyes closed.

At first nothing happened.

There were the usual remarks.

"The spirits are taking their time getting here."

"They've got a long way to come."

"Maybe if everyone would be quiet!"

"You have to be serious if you want to be taken seriously."

"Could everyone please be quiet."

Silence.

Then more remarks.

"The directions on the box say it can take five minutes before anything starts to happen."

"I tried dowsing once and didn't have any luck with that either."

"When is it my turn?"

"Would everyone *please* be quiet?"

Abel Moore watched with mild amusement, thinking: What's the harm? A group of lonely old people hoping that "dead" doesn't really mean dead.

Then his turn—he was paired with Marianna—and the glass began to move.

"Is there a spirit present?" Marianna Reed asked, her voice low.

The glass glided to the upper left-hand corner of the board and stopped at the word: YES.

"You must be pushing," Abel Moore said.

Marianna removed her fingertips from the glass, then whispered, "Who are you?"

Only Abel Moore was touching the glass as it began to glide again. This time it jerked to a stop first at W, then at B, then at Y.

"WBY?" somebody said. "What does that mean?"

Nobody had an answer to that, and after a moment Marianna went on, "Who's the message for?"

The glass took off, jerking disjointedly across the board. It spelled J. QUINN.

There was a stir at the table. One of the guests was Joshua Quinn, a neighbor of Marianna's, a thickset, unassuming man in his fifties, a champion windsurfer.

He spoke up now in a quiet voice. "Find out what the message is."

"What's the message?" Abel Moore didn't wait for Marianna this time, hoping his question was correct procedure.

"For god's sakes," someone said, and one of the women giggled.

"Shhh," someone whispered. "There's a presence in the room."

The group fell silent, waiting. Then, as before, the glass began to jerk around the board, stopping at certain letters, until at last it

produced a sentence. The sentence was MONEY IN WHITMAN SAM-
PLER BOX.

"What money?"

"What Whitman Sampler box?"

"There's something phony about all this."

"Joshua, what *is* this all about?"

"Ask the board," Joshua suggested.

But that was it. The "presence"—if that's what it was—would say no
more. Abel Moore asked another question or two, as did several of the
other guests, but the glass refused to budge.

To ease the tension in the room, Marianna brought out a bottle of
brandy and poured drinks. Joshua Quinn downed his with a preoccu-
pied expression. Then he suggested that the group adjourn to his next
door apartment. The party trooped over, and once there, Joshua began
to hunt in a closet until he found on a shelf what he was looking for.
An old Whitman Sampler candy box. Inside, beneath a pile of old
birthday cards, valentines, a few letters, lay a packet of money, secured
by a rubber band. Hundred-dollar bills. He counted them. Sixty one-
hundred dollar bills. Six thousand dollars.

Six thousand dollars that Joshua Quinn swore he'd never seen before.

Hidden there by whom? Joshua said he'd removed the box from his
mother's apartment after her death. He 'd meant to sort these personal
effects, but never did it. Had his mother put the money there? His grandmother? Joshua could only guess.

That had been the beginning.

The pilot's voice interrupts Abel Moore's drifting thoughts. "We're
flying at twenty thousand feet; visibility's excellent; we should arrive at
Washington National Airport on time, at 1:35 this afternoon. The tem-
perature in Washington is eighty-one degrees."

Abel Moore butters his roll and eats his salad.

Flying at twenty thousand feet. One of those saints—was it Simon?—
claimed the power of flight. Not Simon. Joseph. Joseph of Cupertino.
Not flight exactly. Levitation. A witness swore he saw Joseph of
Cupertino hang in the air for two hours. The nineteenth-century psy-

chic Daniel Home floated in and out of windows. Hawthorne saw him. So did Queen Victoria.

So what?

People who fly.

Animals that talk.

Farfetched, but not impossible. Anything's possible.

Didn't he find—via a Ouija board—six thousand dollars inside an old candy box?

Didn't he follow that up by finding Ellen Kohler, kidnapped from a shopping mall in Gaithersburg, Maryland, when she was six and found three years later living as Melissa James in Baton Rouge, Louisiana. Found by him. Blood tests confirmed it.

His second feat.

Ellen's whereabouts revealed at another session with the Ouija board. This time the message came through when a second cousin of the missing child asked for information. As before, as soon as he touched the glass, it energized. Jumped to life and spelled out the place where Ellen eventually was found.

After that, relatives of missing children, detectives, police officers, journalists flocked to his door. Marianna arranged more sessions with the Ouija board, but the Ouija board seemed to have dried up. Marianna got together a séance where the participants sat around a table, hands joined. Nothing came through. They tried automatic writing, even gazed into soap bubbles in the hope of contacting the spirits.

Nothing.

Still, people didn't give up. Some began to bring in objects belonging to missing kids.

John Kakutani's baseball glove.

Andrea Ausubel's red sweater.

The objects worked. He held them and as with the whisky glass, power surged. He "felt" the history of the object, "saw" into it. He got vibrations. It seemed as if the baseball glove was speaking to him and he could both hear and understand it.

Besides Ellen, in the next year he found Andrea Ausubel, Diane Mercer, Ricky Adler, John Kakutani, and Desiree McKenny. Six missing kids in all, all tracked down thanks to him. Not that finding the kids was always a joyful occasion. It wasn't.

Andrea, Diane, and Ricky were dead.

John Kakutani, found cruising the streets of Atlanta, had left home of his own volition and had no desire to return. Desiree McKenny turned up in California with a boyfriend.

Marianna read in her books and announced, "You're a psychometrist. In the old sense of the word. Not a modern psychometrist who tests and measures. But a nineteenth-century one."

"Tell me more," he said.

"You're 'sensitive' to objects. You sense their vibrations."

"What kind of vibrations?"

"Vibrations caused by thoughts left by an object's owners."

He read up on it himself and discovered an alternate theory. This theory assumed that animals, vegetables, and minerals possess souls. Souls he was sensitive to.

None of it made sense to him.

How had it happened?

He'd never been "sensitive" to souls of objects before. Or to vibrations imprinted by previous owners.

Had something happened during his operation for the tumor? Some dormant part of his brain activated? Like that house painter who slipped off a ladder, lapsed into a coma, and later found himself psychic.

A month after his first success, a doctor measured him for body heat and found his head and torso abnormally hot. As if he were radiating energy or burning with a low grade fever.

Which meant?

Who knew?

In any event, those early cases seemed a million years ago. Seemed like beginner's luck. Now he directs an institute and a staff of three. Now he's known as the foremost psychometrist in the country. Psychometrist in the old sense of the word. People travel from as far away as New Zealand for "readings." They hand him an object and expect him to "sense" the life of its owner.

They hope he can do it.

It isn't all smooth sailing.

His powers work about thirty-three percent of the time. In the past four years he's found thirty more missing children.

Sherlock Holmes may have predicted that the detectives of the future would all be clairvoyants, but that future hasn't arrived yet. Didn't thousands of psychics offer tips during the Atlanta child murder spree in the early 1980s, but none panned out?

That case before his time.

He's fizzled plenty of times. He had no intuitions about the killer who strangled three young women on the Gainesville campus. He failed to get a reading on at least a hundred other missing children. Found thirty-six, failed to find a hundred. When handed an arrowhead, he couldn't "read" the name of the tribe or envision details about the life style of the Indians who centuries earlier had fashioned it.

He hasn't had a successful "reading" in six months.

Still, disciples seek his advice on everything from geological changes to political upheavals to UFO sightings.

People want to believe.

"More coffee?"

Abel Moore nods. He sips the coffee, bites into the cream puff. After the flight attendant removes his tray, he lets his elbow spill even further over the armrest into the next seat. He pulls out a book, but before he even opens it his heavy-lidded eyes droop. Soon they'll arrive. He'll be met by a believer and in the evening lecture to a room full of believers.

People want to believe.

Change your hair color and lose five pounds.

None of this seems possible.

Him a psychometrist!

His idea had been to spend his retirement fishing.

Now he's flying into Washington, D.C. His last visit—twenty-five years ago—had been with Helen and Deb. Deb was ten. They stayed in a motel in Virginia and each day drove into the city. Saw the Hope

Diamond, the Spirit of St. Louis, the statues of Lincoln and Jefferson. Took a barge ride on the C & O canal, pulled by mules.

Now his return as Man of the Hour. The Man Who Sees the Future. Who Uncovers What is Hidden. Flying a thousand miles to speak to a group called the Zoetic Society. For a thousand dollars.

His heavy eyes droop further, the lines in his wide face soften and relax, the big body sprawls, and an hour later, when the pilot announces the approach to Washington's National Airport, the flight attendant has to touch him lightly on the shoulder to awaken him.

ON SATURDAY MORNING, at the Carrol Avenue Swim and Fitness Club, Geneva swims twenty-five laps (Australian crawl and butterfly stroke) in her black tank suit. As she flutters her long legs, she recites to herself: *If I were called in / To construct a religion / I should make use of water.* "Water" by Philip Larkin. She agrees. Water props you up, provides you with the sensation of weightlessness. If it doesn't drown you, it washes you clean, prepares you for a new life.

A new life. One with a job offer. With stable walls. An emotional life that's not frozen. No insomnia. No conviction that she's missed the boat. How did she end up a thirty-one-year-old virgin? She's probably the only one in North America. As exotic as any lake creature. She's had her chances. Danny Tutko in twelfth grade. Gerald Ashenberg in her bibliography seminar. Gerald took her to an Italian restaurant on her birthday. She meant to go to bed with him, but the semester ended before she could do it, and when the new term started, Gerald had disappeared. To enter his father's envelope business, according to the department secretary.

She must restart her stalled life! Poppy, eight years younger, has a child. An absent and an on-the-spot boyfriend. Opal's got a husband, a house, a son. A job with a paycheck. She's survived cancer. They haven't buried themselves in poems and articles and research projects. They have more to show than a black-bound volume entitled "Yeats' Desert Search: A Scorched Soul in a Supernatural Landscape."

Later that afternoon, Geneva composes a letter to Mayor Barry about pot holes in the streets, but in mid-sentence she stops and sighs for the lost Gerald.

The road not taken.

In the basket where she keeps her correspondence, she finds a recipe for Katherine Hepburn's brownies. A recipe someone at a long ago department picnic gave her. She (Marcella Torres? Betty Raffel?) distributed copies of the recipe to everyone present, though no one asked for it. If only she had that kind of self-assurance! But she doesn't. And they weren't even Alice B. Toklas brownies, the ones made with marijuana or hash or whatever it was. Not that she'd know the difference. Another road not taken. Never tried marijuana or hash or speed or crack cocaine. Nothing but the occasional shot of vodka. Now and then more than one shot.

Poppy's probably tried pot. Opal too. Didn't she go to school in the sixties?

How has she, Geneva Elinor Lamb, evolved into such a cautious creature?

Cautious and superstitious. Too superstitious to throw out a Xeroxed copy of a recipe that she doesn't want and will probably never make.

Plenty of other things she'll never do. Roads not taken. She'll never understand Yeats' cyclical theory of history, although she almost understands it. She'll never learn to like yogurt. Or loud music.

She opens her notebook. At the top of the page she reads: "The Esurient Kitty." This is the title of the children's story she intends to write. "Esurient" means greedy. Her idea is to use big words, one big word on every page so that a child will improve her vocabulary without noticing. So far, she's collected some interesting words, although the plot's weak. Actually there is no plot. But her collection of words has potential: "littoral" (a coastal region), "rasorial" (habitually scratching the ground in search of food), "labile" (unstable), "anfractuous" (characterized by intricate windings or turnings), "oneiric" (of or relating to dreams).

If only she could dream up a plot.

She stares at her page for twenty minutes, but no plot materializes.

At five P.M. she showers. She opts for her green silk dress, thinking as she slips it over her head, *Whenas in silk my Julia goes / then, then methinks how sweetly flows / That liquefaction of her clothes.*

"*Liquefaction!*" A possible word?

If she finds a job, she'll need clothes. First the job.

She has to find a job.

She pulls on her scuffed black pumps, careful to slide each foot into the appropriate shoe, since to put a shoe on the wrong foot can bring bad luck.

In front of the mirror she takes stock. Tall, gawky, hair undeniably frizzy. With luck she'll make it through dinner without spilling anything down her front; with luck she'll find people to talk to; with luck no one will notice the scuff marks on her shoes.

A knock at the door.

She opens to a pale young man with close-cropped fair hair and clear-framed glasses.

"Dr. Lamb?"

"I'm Dr. Lamb."

"This came to our house by mistake." He holds out an envelope. "I'm Peter Llanos, staying next door with my aunt."

Geneva takes the envelope, her heart beating at a furious rate. "I believe we spoke on the phone," she says stiffly.

"Right. About the music."

Geneva stands awkwardly, her mind churning with thoughts she dare not express. Then suddenly, inexplicably, her unspoken words boil over, and she finds herself saying in an agitated voice: "Why didn't you turn down your music the other night when you said you would? Why did you throw a rock through my living room window? What's the matter with you? Why have you suddenly become a presence in my life?" She realizes she's shouting and stops as abruptly as she started.

Peter looks mildly surprised. "Sorry to have disturbed you," he says and walks away.

Geneva stands as still as a floor lamp and waits for the pounding in her ribcage to subside. It's important to stay calm. To maintain control.

She visualizes herself in water. Floating. Being lifted. It isn't like her to lose her temper. She can't recall the last time it happened.

Then she remembers the letter. It's from a university in South Carolina. She rips it open, but no job offer.

The first response she's received.

One out of sixty.

Fifty-nine to go.

She tears the letter into pieces and drops them, one by one, into the wastebasket.

Then once again she imagines herself floating, lifted by clear waters, so that ten minutes later when she leaves her cottage, she feels as calm and cool as the water she began the day swimming in.

OPAL BEATS EGG whites to stiff peaks and spreads the mixture on her face. She looks like a moldy strawberry, but the homemade "wrinkle remover" promises to tighten her pores and smooth her skin. She'll leave it on for thirty minutes. Tonight when she introduces Abel Moore, she'll look younger than fifty-nine. Nothing ventured, nothing gained.

After the chemo, she felt she'd aged a year. She stared in the mirror: deeper lines around her mouth, neck flabbier, arms wrinkled. She looked like a blouse left too long in the dryer.

Earlier, Mona Friendly had broached the subject of alternative treatments. "Is this chemo necessary?" she asked in her fluttery way. "Aren't there other possibilities?"

There were. As many alternative therapies as alternative theories for who wrote Shakespeare's plays.

"Those clinics in Mexico," Mona said. "Apricot pits."

"Laetrile. Supposed to stop the cancer from spreading, but no one's proved it."

"Hard to prove things," Mona murmured. "You should investigate."

"I'll do that," she promised. A forest of conflicting claims out there. Shark cartilage. Herb tonics that normalize cell metabolism. Bee venom.

Coffee enemas. A dozen glasses of fruit and vegetable juice a day. The macrobiotic diet: whole grains. Beta-carotene. Acupuncture. Vitamin therapy. Detoxification. Enzyme therapies. Electromagnetic therapy. Castor-oil packs. Colonic therapy. Spiritual de-stressing. Immuno-augmentative therapy. Injections of a substance made from mistletoe, also supposed to enhance your immune system. Testimonials also available on yeast mold derivatives, unsweetened grape juice, barley grass, wheat grass, CO-Q 10.

She looked into them all, but in the end took her doctor's advice and opted for chemo.

Four-and-a-half years later, she swallows vitamins daily, eats broccoli, cabbage, bananas, fish. Includes garlic and ginger in her diet. Olive oil. Tries to avoid red meat, caffeine, alcohol, fats. She'd eat soy products if she could stand them. She drinks bottled water, sprinkles barley grass in her soup, exercises faithfully, practices breathing, meditates.

Upstairs, not wanting to smear egg white on anything, she lies stiffly on the bed. From beneath the Indian bedspread, she extracts a pillow, props up her head, closes her eyes. An article on animal psi for the next *Zoetic Review*? Goldfish that predict earthquakes. Crocodiles that kill by attacking a man's reflection in water.

Too similar to exotic animals in big cities? Animals an overused topic?

Plant psi? Plants communicate by hormones drifting through the air. Potatoes possess precise information about the moon, know whether it's just arisen, has reached its zenith, or is setting.

Mineral psi? The Incas knew the secret for softening stones, but never revealed it. Did the secret involve communication with stones?

She's due at Mona's at five. Her introduction's ready; she's rehearsed it five times. She'll wear her purple outfit.

Impossible to lie completely still.

The first time she had a bone scan they taped her feet together.

As a student, she played a fairy in *A Midsummer Night's Dream*. She wore a kimono. In this production fairyland was Asian. Hers was only a small part, and after her few lines (*I do wander every where, / Swifter than the Moon's sphere; / And I serve the Fairy Queen*), she held a stylized position for two minutes, which felt like two hours. Every muscle ached and she agonized she'd wobble and spoil the tableau.

She stretches her legs and wiggles her toes.

Minor parts. The story of her life. This evening will be no different. She'll deliver three minutes of biography, then step aside.

An article on unusual biographies?

No, her province is the paranormal.

It's what's left over, like the thin line of grit that remains after the rest is swept into the dust pan.

What's left over. Rosalie would scoff. She prefers the solid world, the material, tangible world of old paperweights, old French doorbells, old umbrella handles. Her shop's filled with objects, each containing a history, a style, a "thingness." If told about a sighting of Eleanor Roosevelt on a Formica tabletop and the shrine erected to honor the vision, Rosalie would concentrate on the artifacts. Is the Formica table art deco? Any matching chairs available? An altarpiece from a small Baptist church in a North Carolina mountain community recently sold at local auction for $750.

The house is quiet as a shrine.

Where's Sol? In his studio? Out walking?

He should be getting dressed.

An article on those exploding match boxes in Australia? One on garden hoses that "disappear" into the earth? One on vision stories? Put Eleanor Roosevelt in perspective. Compare her with Amelia Earhart whose fans continued to spot her for years after she disappeared.

Has she misspent her life investigating such matters? What do they add up to? Why does she bother?

Her thoughts drift and she falls asleep.

In her dream, she's going out to dinner with friends. They pass a flight of stairs, and she begins to climb them. She's looking for something, perhaps the ladies' room. The stairs are steep, the opening at the top narrow. She pulls herself through and finds she's in a madcap beauty salon. She sits down to wait for a haircut. Finally everyone leaves, except a bald man and herself. She continues waiting for her haircut.

She wakes up, and the dream slides away, like an egg from a spatula. *Dreams restore the psychic equilibrium and always mean something.*

This one means?

She struggles to remember it.

A dream about hair. Hair signifies thoughts; hair grows outside the head, thoughts grow inside the head. Waiting for a haircut must mean waiting for old thoughts to be sheared away. The bald man? A projection of herself without thoughts?

She's thoughtless?

She's not a deep thinker?

Are these conditions for which a cure exists?

Hair also associated with strength. Look what happened to Samson.

Two weeks after her first chemo treatment, her hair started to fall out. In the mornings, she'd find the pillow covered. Within a week, she was bald. For months, she wore a wig. Like Samson, her energy declined. Like Samson, both hair and energy eventually returned. The one good thing was that when her hair grew back, it grew back curly.

Now she wonders: Will the cancer, like her hair, come back? Every ache or pain is suspicious. A headache. Has the disease metastasized to her brain? A backache. Has it migrated to her bones? Shortness of breath. Is it in her lungs? Significant that she lost three pounds? The icy feeling that enveloped her after a mammogram when the technician called her back for extra pictures. The misgivings before every doctor's appointment.

She checks her watch.

Thoughtless.

Not a deep thinker.

True?

The face mask's been in place for forty-five minutes.

In the bathroom, she rinses off the caked egg white and examines her face.

Her skin seems tauter.

She craves a sign but hasn't been granted one. Already twice today she's checked for a message on the pad by Sol's painting. To no avail. In Italy, in the nineteenth century, a statue of St. Dominic came to life, the event declared a miracle by the local bishop. In *Don Giovanni*, the statue comes to life. In *The Winter's Tale*, the statue comes to life. In *Pygmalion* the statue comes to life. St. Francis? Didn't a statue prompt him to undertake his special mission?

She assembles a Salade Niçoise to take to Mona Friendly's, then showers and dresses. She stares at her—for the moment—unlined face in the mirror and applies eyebrow pencil, but fails to get her eyebrows even. At least she has eyebrows to worry about. Hair. She's no longer dependent on wigs, turbans, scarves. She washes her face and redraws the lines, but the results remain imperfect. In spite of all her practice, she learned nothing. She neither figured out how to tie a scarf nor to produce matching eyebrows. And when she affixes a gold filigree butterfly pin to the collar of her purple blouse, she doesn't get that on straight either.

"ENTROPY. IT'S THE fundamental law of nature. Things run down. Apples rot. Children's rooms get messy, not neat." Dionne Inglenook, a pretty, middle-aged woman, draped in a peach-colored shawl, is the speaker. Her sleek hair sports a geometric cut.

Dionne, like most of Mona Friendly's guests, is a member of the Board.

"*Things fall apart, the center cannot hold,*" Geneva quotes Yeats.

"Disorder's the path of least resistance."

The two women are sipping punch in Mona Friendly's white Cleveland Park garden. White rhododendron, white iris, white peonies.

"May I join you?" asks a small man carrying a plate of hors d'oeuvres.

"Of course, Dr. Westcot." Dionne Inglenook steps back to include him. "We're talking about chaos."

"The tendency towards chaos," Geneva clarifies. "*All the king's horses and all the king's men, couldn't put Humpty Dumpty together again.*"

Dr. Westcot, a short, fierce-looking man in a biscuit-colored suit, bites into a cheese puff. "Do you discount creation, then? Things get made. Order gets established. Skyscrapers get built."

"Never thought of that," Dionne admits.

"Symphonies get composed."

"What about people who try to be helpful?" Dionne Inglenook adjusts her shawl. "The ones in supermarket checkout lines who put the bar across the conveyer belt to separate your groceries from theirs? The ones who return your tennis balls that have landed on their court?"

"Genetic." Dr. Westcot looks around for a place to deposit his plate, but doesn't find one. "Self-sacrificing people like firemen and policemen are born with a certain gene. Those who return tennis balls no doubt harbor a gene for helpfulness."

Geneva can't believe her ears. Can returning mishit tennis balls be a genetic response? If so, she's not prepared to consider it. She retreats a step or two. It's a delicate spring evening; Mona's garden is weeded, mulched, the white blossoms lambent in the fading light. The punch isn't too sweet. She stands alone, appreciating the moment. No need to talk to someone every single minute. Fragments of conversation drift in her direction. "Is it possible to treat bone fractures with electricity?" someone asks. And another voice wants to know whether it's fair to call a crowd a "biological entity."

Abel Moore stands by the French doors and surveys the garden. He's managed a two-hour nap and feels rested. Ready to mix and mingle. That's what they're paying him for. He watches a young woman passing a tray of appetizers, then squares his shoulders and lunges in Geneva's direction. The guest of honor has noticed the tall young woman.

Her bushy hair and awkward stance make him think of a medieval painting where the perspective's off. She seems flat and oversized for the background. Superimposed upon it. Since he feels out of place himself, he sympathizes.

"I don't believe we've met."

"Geneva Lamb."

"Abel Moore."

"I know." Geneva doesn't mean to be unhelpful, but she's at her usual loss.

"You are a member of the Board?"

"I volunteer with the Society." Geneva transfers her punch from her right hand to her left.

"What would we do without volunteers?"

Geneva can't answer that. She feels flattered that Abel Moore has singled her out, but how to capitalize on it? Besides, she's at the Society under false pretenses. She's a skeptic. A disbeliever. Superstitious, but a disbeliever.

Abel Moore senses her reluctance to talk. Unusual among volunteers. Most like nothing better than to give you a few "mind over matter stories." How concentration increased their daughter's bust size. How visualization cured their neighbor's osteoporosis.

Geneva feels taller than usual, which also lessens her self-confidence. Could her diminished conversational skills have caused her body to grow? Why is exchanging a few words with a stranger so difficult? She swishes the punch in her cup. A thin connection flickers between herself and this big man, a thread that can disconnect any second. She wants to do her share but suspects it's hopeless. Why isn't she more vivacious? More charming? She'd give a tooth for an infusion of charm. Why is she thinking so much? Why can't she just relax and react. She knows he's scrutinizing her; he wants to be friendly and so does she! Yet her thoughts lie like matted straw inside her head, too sodden and heavy to transmute into light and golden words.

"I hope you had a pleasant flight up," she says at last, a little desperately.

"Very smooth."

"Have you heard about Eleanor Roosevelt's face on the tabletop?" Idiotic, but maybe this subject will interest him.

Abel Moore has not, and Geneva blurts out the details. She hopes he won't notice that her nails aren't evenly cut, that her dress tends to bunch up on one side, that her shoes are scuffed.

Finally, at wit's end, she asks whether he believes people who return mishit tennis balls have a genetic switch that prompts their actions.

"Mishit tennis balls?" Abel Moore scratches his head. He's not a biologist. How should he know? Genetics? Not his forte. Offhand, he'd say someone who mishits tennis balls probably isn't keeping his eye on the ball. Or isn't getting his racquet back. Or ... but he's drifted off the subject which is someone returning tennis balls to the players on the next court. Doesn't common courtesy account for that? He's about to make this point when Opal arrives, introduces herself, apologizes to Geneva, and drags him away.

Dr. Westcot, who's been edging nearer and nearer, jumps in to fill the void, "It doesn't have to be genetics as we know it. It's possible that words, phrases, theories, and ideas are a kind of nonphysical gene ..."

Geneva produces a thin smile. This is getting worse and worse.

She turns to the hors d'oeuvres tray that Poppy is passing and snatches a stuffed red potato. She nibbles at it. Sour cream. And what are these salty black beads? Like miniature birds' eyes. Caviar. A first. She eats the potato. Delicious. "Nonphysical genes?" Geneva repeats. What's Dr. Westcot talking about?

His listener's lack of comprehension fails to deter Dr. Westcot. "Ideas are alive, they hop from brain to brain."

Geneva mumbles an unintelligible reply and looks around for another potato.

Dr. Westcot presses on. "Nonphysical genes are only one possibility. It could be morphic fields."

"Morphic fields?" Geneva bobs her head hopelessly. This water's too deep; she recognizes the same sinking sensation she felt when first confronted with Yeats' cyclical theory of history.

Dr. Westcot takes her nod as a green light. "For example, different parts of a plant develop differently, although the DNA's exactly the same. The leaves of a plant develop differently from the roots or the stem. The question is, How do leaves 'know' to become leaves? A stem to become a stem?"

"Good question," Geneva admits.

"Couldn't it be that 'things' have memory, and each member of a species draws on the collective memory of its particular group?"

Diane Inglenook, who's been lingering nearby, interrupts, "Any resemblance to Jung's collective unconscious?"

"Exactly!" Dr. Westcot exclaims. "After the first one in a species does something new or learns something new, it's easier for the rest of the group—because of the resonance of the morphic field around the first achiever. It's not too far-fetched to suppose an invisible memory connects all members of the same species, is it?"

"Yeats' Spiritus Mundi," Geneva says, determined to hang in there.

Dr. Westcot fingers his necktie. "There's a creative principle in nature that drives things onward. We see it in the expansion of the universe. We see it in evolution. We see that nature breaks up old patterns and prevents things from stopping where they are. We see that life grows when new opportunities appear, often in the wake of great accidents or cataclysms."

For some reason Geneva feels tears begin in her eyes. She turns away to collect herself. "Life grows when new opportunities appear." How hopeful that sounds! And what he said about an ongoing creative principle in nature! Is it true? If it is, how can she align herself with such a principle? How allow it to sweep her into new opportunities, open her to new life, infuse her with new energy, establish in her a new harmony with the vast outside world that so often seems alien and unknowable.

"GET YOU ANYTHING?" Opal takes a good look at the Miracle Man. If that's what he is. What did she expect? A small, wiry, exercise guru type, wearing tennis shoes? A grey-haired ascetic, pale eyes glittering with esoteric wisdom? Anything but this oversized, unspiritual-looking, awkward man.

"No thank you, I'm fine."

"Wine?" Opal gestures to a waiter carrying a tray of drinks.

"No, no." Abel Moore turns from the waiter. Save the wine for after the lecture. Now's the time to stay alert. Clear-headed. "I think the Zoetic Review's a solid little magazine." Mild flattery that couldn't deceive a fly. But he does read the publication. Cover to cover.

"Thanks." Someone appreciates her efforts. Or maybe he's just being polite. "Your piece generated more commentary than any we've ever run." Almost true. That article on the moving cemetery monument in Marion, Ohio, elicited more response.

"I'm astonished."

"A dozen letters. I'll forward them to you."

"I'd love to see them!"

"Usually an article generates two or three responses." Opal rubs the grass with her shoe. "You're proof miracles still happen." If what Moore pulled off was a miracle.

"Miracles," he repeats. The waiter with the tray of wine glasses nears and Abel Moore takes a glass of red. A sip won't hurt. He needs to relax. He'll just wet his lips.

He brushes away a passing moth. "Miracles are like small animals in the forest. Sometimes you see them, but mostly you don't." Miracle. The word should be excised from the language. A shape can turn inside out in an instant. Like a coat. Trees solidify into petrified wood. As for his performance tonight … it remains to be seen. He could bomb. It's happened before.

"I hope I'll be lucky," he says.

"If luck is with you, even your ox will give birth to a calf." One of her mother's proverbs.

"Exactly." If only he can remember to go for the real thing. Not for the effect.

She smiles. Meeting new people. Will they reveal a flash of their true spirit or not? At age twenty-five, every new encounter seemed a brave new world. But now the masks are fixed in place. Harder to get someone to lift even a corner.

She takes a deep breath. "How do you do it?"

Abel Moore sips his wine. The question that's always lurking. "I wish I knew. My theory is that there's a universal mind and sometimes I tap into it. What I mean by universal mind is … think of a star with billions of points. The center of the star corresponds to the universal mind while the points of the star correspond to individual minds."

"We're all connected to the universal mind—"

"But you can't force it. Just because there are white threads in my hair doesn't mean I can weave a shirt with them."

Opal looks a little startled. What does that mean? "What did Joshua Quinn do with the money he found?" she asks to keep the conversation going.

"No idea. But he counted it twice, touching each bill as if it were a dried leaf that might disintegrate any instant."

"I would have done the same."

"It was as if he—as if all of us in that room—had somehow stumbled upon the secret of secrets."

Opal smiles. Secret of secrets. Pretentious. But interesting. This Abel Moore reminds her of someone waiting for a foot race to begin. He's preparing for the competition. Warming up. Shortly the gun will go off. When that happens, he'll bolt into action. Flee beyond her horizon.

His smile, which answers hers, contains a shade of irony.

A moment of connection.

"What's upcoming in the magazine?" Abel Moore asks and the moment slides away. What is she thinking? Opal Kirschbaum, his correspondent for the last six months. The editor of his article. This is her show. She's checking him out. Can't blame her. He'd do the same. Hope he doesn't disappoint her. Any way to get rid of this wine glass? It's still half full. He glances around for inspiration, and in the process notices Geneva talking to Dr. Westcot. "That young lady," he gestures in Geneva's direction, "mentioned an apparition of Eleanor Roosevelt. Is that the subject of a future article?"

"Not in the next issue," Opal says offhandedly, as if she knows exactly which articles will appear in the next issue. "All we've heard are reports on the radio."

"Ah!"

"We're considering an article on Swallowing Vitamins Can Make You a Winner at the Racetrack."

At this moment, Mona Friendly, willowy in a dress the color of sea foam, appears to announce that dinner's ready.

MONA FRIENDLY, HER thin face leathery, golden hair tucked behind her ears, gathers her guests. The lecture begins at eight P.M. Against the pink-gold sky, the long table draped in a white cloth and sprouting silver candelabra like rams' horns looks like a becalmed Viking ship.

Since Mona's talents aren't culinary, a catering firm has provided the dinner, although a few guests have contributed salads. "It's food for thought that interests me," is one of her self-definitions.

Abel Moore is seated between Mona and Opal.

Mona addresses the guest of honor. "Your reputation in the psychic field is second only to Edgar Cayce's. My grandmother had a reading by Cayce."

"What did he tell her?" Abel Moore politely asks.

"Eat local vegetables. Eat almonds."

"Almonds are anti-carcinogenic," Opal says.

"What else did he tell your grandmother?" Abel Moore persists.

"That she had a 'masculine' cast of mind. That in a previous life she lived as a male. Her husband claimed that's where she got the urge to run things."

"I'm not sure the urge to run things is a male trait," Poppy interjects from the other end of the table.

Opal looks around. Except for Sol, Poppy, and Geneva, all the guests are members of the Board. Besides Diane Inglenook and Dr. Westcot, there's Mabel Sullivan, a heavy-set woman about seventy, a physician whose specialty is holistic medical practices. Her husband, Nathan, once an electrical engineer, now spends his days worrying about whether increased electrical activity in the environment causes headaches and allergic reactions. The most exotic-looking guest (black ponytail, silver ankh-shaped earring) is Barry Marcus, a self-styled philosopher and promoter of psychic fairs. And next to Geneva sits Nevil Prokofiev, a distant relative of the composer and minister in a local psychic church.

The food arrives: a large, decorated platter of cold salmon, bowls of salads, baskets of rolls, bottles of wine.

"Half a glass," Abel Moore instructs when a server offers.

Opal sticks to water.

She takes it all in. Sol's discussion with Mabel Sullivan about the stock market. Poppy's conversation with the psychic fair impresario who radiates self-confidence. Geneva's interchange with Nevil Prokofiev, a man with pale skin and a short black beard, during which she blurts out in a voice that's a little too loud, "I've heard so many interesting things about your church!"

"We're offering a course in developing your psychic awareness."

On her other side, Abel Moore repeats for Mona Friendly the details of finding the six thousand dollars inside the candy box. Across the table, Dionne Inglenook adjusts her shawl as she speaks with Nathan Sullivan. Opal hears the word "shingles," a condition she knows Dionne recently suffered. Nathan Sullivan, erect in a pale blue sports jacket and sprightly yellow tie, listens in a lively and alert manner. He's over eighty, but a few blond, metallic-looking streaks still glint in his thick white hair. His blue eyes blaze as he talks. He doesn't look like a man who goes to dialysis three times a week.

The walking wounded at this table.

Except for Poppy and Geneva, everyone well over fifty.

Subject to breakdown.

Barry Sullivan underwent laser surgery on his right eye for glaucoma.

Dr. Westcot takes insulin for diabetes.

Two years ago Mona suffered a bout of Bell's Palsy, which left half her face paralyzed, though the condition is hardly noticeable now.

Mabel Sullivan with fibromyalgia.

And Nevil Prokofiev. A hip replacement in 1990.

Sol's string of ailments. A broken molar from biting into a hard candy, a fish bone in his throat, a pulled ligament that kept him off the tennis court for months, a stiff arm from moving Rachel's marble table, sinusitis.

Her cancer.

Nearly five years ago.

Since then, the world seems rented.

Abel Moore looks healthy enough.

At that moment the guest of honor turns to her and says, "Did you know that my powers developed after an operation for a brain tumor?"

Opal picks at her salmon. Filled with tiny, nearly invisible bones, thin and sharp as pins. That time Sol became convinced (in the middle of the night) that a halibut bone from dinner remained in his throat. He couldn't breathe; the bone had pierced the soft lining of his throat;

he could almost taste blood. At the emergency room, the doctor discovered no bone. Sol insisted he felt it. The physician looked again, but found nothing. *Only the sensation of a bone*, the physician assured him. *Not a real bone. A sensation, an imprint, a phantom. You're choking on a phantom bone.*

A red cabbage salad is handed to her, and Opal fills her plate. Beta carotene. Believed to be anti-carcinogenic. Abel Moore, she notes, dips into every plate and bowl. He tries the salmon (so he's not a vegetarian); he tries her Salade Niçoise.

"I'd like to see an article on TV psychics," Mona says. "One claims his contact is a dead seven-year-old girl."

"Anything's possible," Abel Moore says diplomatically.

Dr. Westcot licks his lips and enters the conversation. "The influence of a dead child is as possible as the influence of extinct species … or of their morphic fields. Some believe that memories aren't stored in the brain, but in morphic fields. The brain acts like a TV receiver and tunes in to them, and, at death, when the brain decays, the memories and ideas continue to survive."

Opal crunches salad and butters a roll.

"Morphic fields." Mona Friendly hitches a shoulder pad inside her willowy dress. "I'm unfamiliar with that terminology."

Dr. Westcot looks to Abel Moore for support.

"Continue," the guest of honor urges.

Dr. Westcot looks embarrassed. He talks too much, a lifelong failing. But … he's been asked. In a respectful tone, he mentions Sheldrake, the author of the theory. "Essentially what he's saying is that the form of things is controlled not by DNA but by surrounding morphic fields. And these morphic fields have a built-in memory of how similar things are formed."

"I've heard of this theory." Abel Moore says. "Everything has a morphic field, right? People. Potatoes. Rats. Social groups. Crystals. Atoms. A crystal spontaneously crystallizes just like a tomato plant spontaneously grows. In a sense, a crystal 'remembers' how to become a crystal. Isn't that it?"

Dr. Westcot nods.

Abel Moore drains his half glass. "The point is, everything's alive. Everything's got an inner life."

POPPY STANDS IN Mona Friendly's bathroom, counting to ten. She's already splashed cold water on her face, and now she's intoning in a whisper, "one … two … three." Taking deep breaths between the numbers. I'm calming down, she thinks, I'm not going to start shouting at that … that jerk! Her determination not to "lose it" with Barry Marcus, Mr. Hotshot impresario of the local Psychic Fairs scene, has almost assumed a shape. The shape, however, is not a definable one; it shifts like a cloud, like billows of smoke.

That lunatic actually said, "In ancient Greece, women counted their age from the date of their marriage. Not from their birth. The wedding marked the beginning of a woman's real life. Makes a certain kind of sense, don't you think?"

"No," she said. "I *don't* think."

And in the next breath excused herself.

Because she hadn't wanted to say something rude to Mona's guest. Embarrass herself. Embarrass Opal. Tell Mr. Barry Marcus, with his ponytail, his earring, his love beads, his fringed shirt, to go shove it in his ear.

Mona's bathroom is gorgeous. Black marble walls, a shower curtain that looks like a tapestry, a little antique table by the tub heaped with books and magazines. An assortment of expensive-looking bottles and jars and brushes. Track lighting. A plant stand with an orchid spike in bloom.

She pats her hands dry on a tiny guest towel that's decorated with satin roses.

She fishes in her shoulder bag for her lipstick, applies some, then rubs her lips together to spread the color. All the while thinking, Why me? Why do I always end up with the Neanderthals? What rock did this guy crawl out from under, anyway?

She smoothes her hair. She's feeling better now, calmer, beginning to see the humor. Putting women in their place. Nothing new there. Haven't men been at it for centuries? Look at the famous couples: Jack and Jill, Dick and Jane, Romeo and Juliet, Adam and Eve, Hansel and Gretel, Anthony and Cleopatra, Sonny and Cher—the man always first. Always Number One.

Jerks.

No point getting shrill. That's why she came in here in the first place. To give her sharp thoughts space and time and quiet in which to even out. To relax them. Nothing to be gained from the shrill voice. Nor from shrieking or screaming. All words, she knows, associated almost exclusively with women.

"Poppy! Are you all right?" The question is followed by a soft knock on the door.

"I'm fine," she whispers back. "Out in a minute."

She flings one last look at herself in the mirror. To make sure she's still there, still substantial.

Opens the door.

Geneva stands awkwardly in her green silk dress. "You jumped up so suddenly."

"Something caught in my throat," Poppy says lightly. "All clear now."

Back at the table a general discussion continues. Something about the dangers in the environment from the low-frequency radio waves that emanate from beacons and other sources, the fields produced by high voltage lines, the continual bombardment by transmitters, satellites, CB radios, microwaves, metal detectors, cordless phones, walkie-talkies, garage-door openers.

Poppy half listens. Will Metro grow up in a world where leukemia and deformities have become the norm? Will he, like Nathan Sullivan, become convinced that increased electrical activity in the environment is causing his headaches, his loss of appetite, his restlessness?

She sits at the table, in Mona's pleasant spring garden, among people she barely knows. She knows Opal and Geneva, but not the others. She's met them a few times, listened to their stories as they listened to her tell about her rescue at Chadwick's, but their sitting together tonight seems accidental. Abel Moore especially seems distant and strange. She watches him now, at the head of the table, the man of the hour.

For a minute she closes her eyes, lets the conversation swim around her. It's like she's in a dream, and wouldn't it be something if when she opens her eyes, everything would be gone, Barry Marcus with his ponytail and chauvinistic remarks, Dr. Westcot who keeps licking his lips, even well-meaning Geneva, if all of them simply evaporated and she'd be left alone here with the white iris, the white peonies, the white rhododendron.

She opens her eyes.

The evening light falls gently on the party in the garden.

One of the servers begins clearing the plates, another brushes crumbs away with a silent butler. Mona Friendly checks her watch; dessert and coffee must materialize in five minutes.

A pulse beats in Poppy's forehead, the grass is hard underneath her feet, the dinner guests around the table are turning into silhouettes. Mabel Sullivan's diamond ring sparkles in the pale light. Barry Marcus' silver earring glitters. The setting sun softens the garden, bathes in warm amber the wine glasses, the paving stones of the patio, the tassels on Dionne Inglenook's shawl.

Nevil Prokofiev leans towards Geneva, the two of them deep in some private conversation.

Poppy sits solidly in her chair with the solid ground beneath her, but she feels as if she could be floating. In her head, she's floating. She's light as a feather or a cloud, not attached to anything in this garden unless it's those pale iris, those feathery peonies, those stately rhododendron.

She sits still, balanced, as if the slightest movement could tip her backwards and she'd fall off the edge of the world.

OVER DESSERT (STRAWBERRIES and biscotti) Dionne Inglenook asks Abel Moore his opinion about a well-known psychic who claims a ninety percent accuracy rate.

"Remarkable." Abel Moore reaches for a strawberry. His percentage is thirty-three percent. What's worse, he hasn't had a successful reading in six months and might never have one again. Nor has he been tested. Forget those Florida professors who handed him fossil remains and moon rocks and asked for his impressions. Impressions he didn't have. If that was a test, he failed it. One of many failures.

"She predicted the Los Angeles earthquake of 1994."

"Good for her!"

"She predicted that China would launch a nuclear attack in 1992!"

"Can't win em all." Failure always possible. Sometimes a flower has scent, sometimes not. All the missing children he hasn't found. The one hundred children he hasn't found.

Dionne Inglenook rubs a water spot on her spoon with her napkin. "Many of us have questions. Will you be giving any readings?"

"I hope to." Successful readings or failures? That's the question. That's what he can't predict. He dips a strawberry in powdered sugar. If only he can remain positive. Not think too much. Too much thinking interferes. Nice shawl this lady's wearing. An aunt of his had one like it fifty years ago and even then it looked old-fashioned. Same pale color, same silky tassels, same sense that wearing it signified an important occasion.

Time is growing shorter, and several at the table want to squeeze in questions while they still have a chance. A server pours coffee from a silver pot. Mabel Sullivan takes two lumps of sugar and asks, "Are you familiar with the Central Premonitions Registry? It's an outfit in New York that collects premonitions about disasters—train wrecks, plane crashes, explosions. Any catastrophe. They solicit forecasts and match them with the actual events when they occur."

"Never heard of em."

Barry Marcus leans forward. "Did you hear about the psychometrist who developed cirrhosis of the liver after picking up the briefcase of a man who had the disease? Could this happen?"

"I don't think so."

"According to the *New York Times* the tendency towards spirituality is an attempt to maximize human potential," Dionne interjects.

"Could be." Why do people assume he's the Delphic Oracle? If the *New York Times* reports it, it's probably true.

"Would the sensation of a bone in the throat be related to morphic fields?" The questioner is Opal. "If someone had a bone in his throat and the impression of it, the memory of it, remained after the bone was gone—"

But it's time to go. Mona stands up and the others follow. As Abel Moore waits for directions, he overhears Mona giving Nathan Sullivan Edgar Cayce's recipe for Mummy Food, a concoction made with dates. Mummy Food! What a high-minded woman! She probably reads Egyptian! That young girl who passed the hors d'oeuvres is staring at the rhododendrons. And Geneva Lamb. She's standing awkwardly, a fish out of water. His counterpart.

The moon, pale as biscotti, has already risen. A professor once gave him a moon rock to hold but he failed to identify it. Not a single impression of moon or space formed. It could happen tonight. No way to guard against a washout. If he were a betting man, he'd say his chances were fifty-fifty.

OPAL EXITS IN step with Barry Marcus. "Is there a psychic fair coming up?" she asks.

"In July. We're featuring a speaker who was abducted by a UFO."

"No kidding!" She's never heard of a UFO abduction she believed in. Probably a case of hysteria. Or fraud. But no one's asked her opinion.

Over the years she's visited dozens of psychic fairs. Wandered among the healing stones, the crystals, sugalites, tiger eyes, amethysts. During her treatment, she carried an amethyst at all times. She usually buys dripless candles at these fairs. A package of herb tea. Once some Chinese exercise balls. She likes the taped music, the displays of books, the intense but laid-back vendors and practitioners. She likes the assumption permeating the air that each person present leads a life filled with simple and deep truths.

What's amazing is that Barry Marcus earns a living from psychic fairs. How good a living she doesn't know. But a living. The other Board members don't depend on their psychic involvements for income.

Mabel Sullivan is a physician with a medical practice; her husband collects a pension; Mona is a rich widow; Dionne Inglenook receives alimony and rents her basement apartment to students. Dr. Westcot, once a professor of history, depends on a retirement plan and social security; Nevil Prokofiev's inheritance from his grandmother financed his church.

The Society issues her a paycheck, but there's Sol's income to fall back on.

"Hope to see you there," Barry Marcus says.

She promises to come.

At the curb a discussion zigzags between Dr. Westcot and Poppy.

From Dr. Westcot: "Our society is future oriented. We're attracted by the idea of progress, the idea of a perfect future, as opposed to a past golden age. For example, in the natural world, the acorn or the oak seedling is drawn towards its formal attractor, its morphic attractor, the mature oak tree."

"What does 'attractor' mean?" Poppy asks.

"The attractor is what Aristotle called the entelechy. Entelechy is the aspect of the soul which is the end that draws everything to it."

"That's not a big help." Attractor. Entelechy. Words she needs to write down. Look up.

"There's the presence of the past in the world around us. And the future also makes itself known. What I'm saying is that nature is not a machine governed by fixed laws, it's more like a developing organism, it has habits, it's alive."

A developing organism. One that's alive. This she understands. "Sounds like Gaia."

Abel Moore walks up and Dr. Westcot excuses himself to usher the guest of honor to his car. The other guests, all conscious of the time, follow suit.

"WHAT DID YOU think of Abel Moore?" Opal asks as Sol maneuvers away from the curb.

"Didn't talk to him."

Sol shifts into second, checks the dashboard for the light switch. He's driving Opal's car, with which he's less familiar.

"Half of him doesn't believe it," Opal says.

Sol finds the lights and turns them on. "I read an article about a man who was blind from birth. Surgery as an adult enabled him to see and overnight his world changed. The spaces between branches of a tree appeared to him like flashing lights! He had a terrible time adjusting. Maybe Moore's in the same boat. Didn't he become psychic late in life?"

"He did."

The street's nearly empty, the sky a neutral grey. A Honda in front of them creeps along, but when Sol tries to pass, the driver speeds up.

"Damn!"

He'd made no effort to talk to Abel Moore because ... because ... he doesn't know why. Abel Moore's like some unidentified bird that's flown into his backyard. A bird he's never seen before. What could it be? A junco? A pine siskin? He needs to creep closer and observe. He needs to match what he's seeing with a picture in a field guide.

But he'd only watched the psychometrist across the table. The man who'd performed extraordinary acts.

If he'd done them.

Could be illusion.

Again Sol moves left to pass; again the Honda speeds up.

"Bastard," he says bitterly. He glances at Opal who's slouched against the door, eyes half closed, rehearsing her introduction.

Illusion. Like those intersecting boxes children draw. If you stare at one long enough, the perspective shifts and the far square becomes the near one.

At a stop sign, he notices a dark shape hovering in a tree, but suddenly it takes wing and disappears over the housetops. Ah, if only something in him, the cautious, the unflying part, could suddenly soar and disappear like that fierce-looking dark bird. Then the ordinary would come to life, the patches of grey sky between branches would shimmer with light, the lit squares of windows would vibrate with radiance, as would the circles of light on approaching cars.

He flashes his headlights at the Honda, which again speeds up.

He honks his horn.

Opal opens her eyes and sits up. "No wonder you have high blood pressure."

"Son of a bitch shouldn't be allowed on the road."

He begins to tailgate the Honda, which honks its horn before turning left at the next intersection.

"Blow it out your ass!" Sol shouts.

After a moment of silence, he says, "Your motor seems a little rough. When was the last time you had this car serviced?"

Opal, reviewing her introduction, doesn't answer.

"The idle's too high."

"The car's fine."

Sol drives another block. "No it isn't. The automatic choke isn't cutting off. Can't you hear it?"

"I don't hear anything."

"Listen. My foot's not on the accelerator. It shouldn't be roaring like that. It's not adjusted properly."

"I just had it tuned up a few weeks ago. When I had the thirty-thousand-mile checkup."

"It doesn't sound right." Sol stops at a red light and inclines his head, listening. He engages the emergency brake and kicks the accelerator. The noise decreases. "See, now the choke's disengaged." He listens. "But, it's not right. It's surging. It should be a steady hum."

"For god's sake, Sol. The car's all right."

"It's not all right. The motor shouldn't sound like this. Listen to it! Can't you hear it pulsing? It's going on and off, on and off. If they tuned it up, they didn't adjust it properly. It should go back."

Opal stares out the window.

The light turns green, Sol releases the emergency brake, and they drive on.

"Can't you hear it? The motor's running too high."

"I don't think it does that when I drive it."

"Do you still have the bill?"

"I think so."

"Maybe I can take it in for you next week. You can use my car."

"Let's worry about it next week."

"It probably only needs a minor adjustment."

"I need to think about my introduction." Opal's tone is stiff.

"Sorry."

They drive in silence for a few blocks, but this time Opal is aware of the motor, which does sound louder than normal. Not that she'd admit it to Sol.

Inside her mind, she recites: "It gives me great pleasure this evening to introduce to you Abel Moore." She envisions herself in front of a room of people. Most seats are taken. Anticipation laces the air.

Sol drives directly to the entrance of the Holiday Inn. "You can get out here. I'll park and catch up."

"Thanks." She gathers her things and opens the door.

Sol addresses the back of her head, "I wouldn't tell you something was the matter with your car if it wasn't true. No need to shoot the messenger."

"Sorry," she says, exiting the car.

THE HOLIDAY INN is swarming. Besides Abel Moore's lecture, the announcement board mentions a wedding, a meeting of a numismatic group, and a singles dance.

Opal hurries to the second floor—the Jefferson Room—where a hundred grey metal folding chairs face a small stage. Banquet tables covered with blue cloths line two walls; the carpeting and draperies are also blue. Just inside the door two card tables have been set up for the ticket sales. The stage holds a lectern and a little table with a pitcher of water and a glass. A microphone coils from the top of the lectern like a cobra.

Opal bends over the microphone. "This is Opal Kirschbaum. O-pal Kirsch-baum." When Poppy and Geneva enter a moment later, she shouts, "Am I loud enough?"

"Loud enough," Poppy calls back.

Geneva fishes an Indian cloth out of a canvas bag, and Poppy helps her spread it over the card tables. Then Geneva sets out a shoebox filled with the pre-ordered tickets, a clipboard with a list attached, and a cash box.

Poppy drags over a couple of the folding chairs, and as soon as Geneva sits down, two people walk up to claim their tickets. A minute later Poppy settles in and two more people show up. In two more minutes it's a steady stream.

Opal hovers as Geneva and Poppy take money and checks, cross names from the list, distribute tickets.

Someone calls her name.

It's Edwina Poole, an old lady with white hair swirled around her head like frozen custard on a cone. Edwina, a Theosophist, explained to Opal on their first meeting that she believed all religions hold the same tenets: a belief in a Supreme Being, a belief that mankind is immortal, a belief that the serious student can unearth divine secrets, a belief that evolution eventually will lead to a developed consciousness.

Tonight Edwina sports an off-the-shoulder blouse, skin-tight black stretch pants, and an amber necklace with smoky orange beads as big as quails' eggs.

"Love your necklace," Opal says.

"Real amber. I had it verified at the Smithsonian. You're only as old as you feel," Edwina goes on, defensive about her outfit. "And I feel forty, not seventy-five. The article on Abel Moore in your magazine mentions he's a widower. That his powers developed after his wife's death. Have you met him yet? Is he good-looking? Still single?"

"Yes to all of the above." It's irritating to feel older than this old woman.

"I can't wait! Will he help us find lost things? A pair of diamond earrings that belonged to my great-grandmother has been missing for two generations. I'm hoping Abel Moore can give me a tip on locating them."

"He's promised to do readings."

People keep streaming in and the center section begins to fill. Edwina raises an eyebrow. "I'm off to grab a seat."

An old gentleman with red eyes sits down in the third row and pulls out a magazine. A thin young woman who moves like a cat whispers conspiratorially to her companion, a young man with a silver ring on every finger.

Angelica Fairfax, a woman with mahogany skin and a wild gleam in her eye, comes up. "Nice turnout." She drapes a black silk jacket on the seat next to the red-eyed man who sits reading, then pats an empty seat and beckons Opal. "I want to show you something." She flutters a newspaper article extracted from her pocketbook. "An article about a woman who's proven that William Shakespeare was really Queen Elizabeth. She compared their facial structures on her computer and it's conclusive. She demonstrates that their left eyes are identical, and that there's an amazing resemblance between their foreheads and chins."

"She's a computer analyst?"

"Also an artist. She established that the Mona Lisa is a self-portrait of Leonardo de Vinci."

"I'd like the article for the files."

Angelica hands it over. "I have another one to show you. After the lecture."

A sturdy woman in opaque stockings and white sandals moves from the middle of the room to the second row, saying, "My eyesight isn't what it used to be."

An old man pushes an old woman in a wheelchair about halfway down.

"Where do you want to sit?" he asks.

"Near where you sit."

"Well, I want to sit right here." He looks at an aisle seat as if thinking about sitting down, but remains standing.

"You know," he says, "I've got pains in both my arms. That's what happened when I had that heart attack."

The old woman says nothing.

"I may have to leave before this is over," the man says.

"Before it's over?"

"Yes. I'm not feeling well. I just told you."

"Let's go now then."

"There's no reason for you to go. You'll enjoy this. I could sit down-stairs in the lobby and come back for you when it's over."

"No, if you're going, I want to go too."

"You'd like to hear this."

"Not if you're thinking about going."

"Okay. Let's go then."

He turns her around, wheels her back up the aisle, stops to ask for a refund, which Geneva provides. Then they're out the door.

A young man does a few neck rolls and says to no one in particular, "Do the lights in here seem too bright?"

Opal tries to count the house, but each time gets a different number. It's like trying to balance her checkbook.

At eight P.M. Dr. Westcot enters with Abel Moore. They take seats in the first row.

A ruddy-looking young man hovers around Poppy as she stows her things. The botanist? Robert? Rupert? Whatever his name is, his tanned skin looks out of place in this crowd devoted to the spiritual and the invisible.

Opal watches Geneva close the doors in back and settle into the last row. As she checks her watch one last time, a latecomer arrives. A plump woman who scurries into a seat next to Geneva and begins a conversation.

Her neighbor? But where's the nephew who likes loud music?

Opal climbs onto the platform and overlooks the crowd. Dionne Inglenook is wrapped in her peach-colored shawl, an expectant expres-sion on her face. Sol is sitting with Mabel and Nathan Sullivan. Opal knows most of the audience; the world of those interested enough in psychic phenomena to attend a lecture isn't extensive.

She touches the microphone.

The doors push open again.

Another latecomer.

Her eyes widen. It's George Bluestone, their upstairs neighbor.

"ON BEHALF OF The Zoetic Society, I'd like to welcome you." Opal assumes her master of ceremonies voice. This is her big moment. She's center stage. She smoothes her purple skirt.

"Our speaker this evening is Abel Moore. His article in last fall's *Zoetic Review* is the reason most of you are here. In it he describes how he found six thousand dollars inside a candy box."

She clears her throat before detailing Abel Moore's late-blooming career. His finding of vanished children, his articles, his awards, his grants, his upcoming workshop. She reminds her listeners that at the reception, after the lecture, issues of the *Zoetic Review* will be on sale, especially the one containing Moore's article.

Finally she steps down and Abel Moore mounts the platform. The audience applauds.

Opal watches him. The psychometrist blots his face with a handkerchief. He stands determinedly, an oversized man in slightly wrinkled clothes.

This better be good, she thinks.

Abel Moore blinks, then begins to speak in a bright, energetic voice. "Let's start by considering chi. You know what chi is, don't you? It's the life force, or the life source, the fundamental energy." He pauses, his eyes scanning the room like a searchlight. "It's a simple concept. Simple and beautiful! American Indians called it manitou, Reich called it orgone energy, Hindus call it prana. Are you listening? It's the universal life energy, I'm talking about. If you do breathing exercises, you experience it as a tingling sensation. When transmitted through the hands, it causes healing. Now don't get confused. Keep your eye on the ball. Manitou, orgone energy, prana—all aliases for that energy, that chi. In other cultures it's known as mana, spiritus, ether, walenda."

Opal fidgets. Nothing new here, which doesn't seem to bother Abel Moore, who hauls out further synonyms: bioenergy, telesma, baraka, odic force.

Abel Moore waves an arm as if he would draw his listeners closer. His voice gets louder. "Listen to me! Energy! It's the most basic concept! When you're talking about energy, you're hitting deep in the court! You know that nature is filled with invisible energies. Think of gravitation. Think of radio waves. Our job is to stay in tune with these energies, and when we do, we feel healthy. But when these energies are blocked, our health suffers."

This Opal believes. During chemo, the days when she felt like something the cat dragged in, she could imagine her chi, her lifeforce—whatever you wanted to call it—as under attack. The nurse, the doctor, all the books and manuals and pamphlets she collected on the subject, swore chemo wasn't as bad as it used to be, but what did they know? It was like morning sickness or sea sickness. That queasy stomach. She took the prescribed pills, but they didn't help. Her stomach lifted to her mouth, she felt green, she felt grey. She couldn't eat the saltines Sol brought her. She tried chicken soup, but couldn't keep it down. A grey choppy sea had moved inside her. She went to bed, but couldn't find a comfortable position.

On the third day Zach stopped by. "How's it going?"

"Not good."

"I have a little present." He handed her a sealed envelope. Stuffed inside were a Ziploc bag of pot and a pack of cigarette papers.

"Supposed to be good for nausea."

"Thanks, sweetie. What a thoughtful gift."

She had to explain to Sol what it was.

The gift cheered her up. She might be old, haglike, nauseated, green, but once she'd been hip. And someone remembered.

And the next day she felt a little better.

Abel Moore speaks without notes, but his words flow like water. His eyes glitter as if they've siphoned off some of the energy he's talking about. "Listen to me! This is important! The chi's inside of you, but that's not all. This chi, this energy, isn't all dressed up with no place to go. It goes here. It goes there. It goes everywhere. It's outside of you, it's in the earth, in the very ground you walk on, and when it's in the ground, it's called earth energy. That's right, earth energy. A thousand years ago, when our ancestors built their places of worship, they built them on hotspots. Hotspots! That's where lines of earth energy intersect. And they buried their dead in the same kinds of places. Where earth energy was concentrated. Where they could feel the chi. Concentrated earth energy is what lies beneath holy wells and holy trees. You can find it on mountaintops. In rivers. Often earth lights are reported at these spots of concentration."

Brenda looks blank when Geneva leans over and whispers, "*The force that through the green fuse drives the flower.* Dylan Thomas." Who is Dylan Thomas? Why does Geneva always sound as if she's reading from a book? But earth lights is an interesting topic because once in Texas she saw them. She was seventeen years old, at the lake. Tiny, diamondlike points of light, flickering over the water. Insects, someone said. Gases from underground streams, someone else explained. Nevertheless, she'd seen them. Tiny, dancing lights, like a spray of water. An electrified spray of water.

"Try this," the big man instructs. "Hold the tips of your fingers together, then pull them apart." He brings his big hands together like a child playing cat's cradle. "This is a special kind of prayer! See the light streaming from your finger ends. That's it! That's the chi! The life force! Pull your fingers slowly apart, and you'll see it. One in three can see it. Radiant energy! The treasure of light!"

Obediently, most members of the audience press their fingers together and pull them apart. Poppy does it and as she draws her fingers away from each other, she sees what seems an arcing band of light.

Russell watches her. That afternoon he took ten hikers to Dyke's Marsh, a shallow swamp beside the Potomac. The still-as-glass water, the cattails, the wild iris. A spit of land jutting into the river. They'd

seen osprey, black duck, blue-winged teal. If the life force was anywhere, it was there.

Abel Moore blots his forehead again. His voice is bright and hyp-
notic, his eyes shining and intense. "Remember now, what's important
here is that the chi of the mind and the chi of the earth are hard to tell
apart. Aren't objective and subjective opposite sides of a coin? Isn't the
part equivalent to the whole? What our ancestors had in mind when
they constructed stone monuments where currents of earth energy collected, was that their stones, like acupuncturists' needles, would tap
the flow of energy beneath."

The psychic unhurriedly pours himself a glass of water and drinks it.
He loosens his tie. "Now I'm going to ask you to take one step further!
Only one step, but remember, one step is more efficient than two! Are
you following me? Not only is the life force found in holy waters, on
mountaintops, and within each individual, but it's buried in every object. Take a rock, for example; rocks record the history of the world,
though only a geologist knows how to read them. We psychometrists
are like geologists."

Rocks, Sol thinks. Alive? Not unchanging, not dead at the center?
Out of nowhere an itch starts in his throat, and he unwraps a cough
drop and pops it in his mouth. A woman turns around and gives him a
dirty look which he pretends not to notice. He won't make a sound.
Absolute silence is possible if one is committed to it. That time on a
skiing trip when four couples shared the living room of an old farm-
house—and he and Opal ... but that was thirty years ago.

Objects alive? Opal thinks. True or false? Her mother's old proverb
pops into her mind: *If God wills it, even a broom can shoot.* Is he talking
about prophetic portraits, malicious automobiles, magical pencils, hungry mirrors, violins with heartbeats? Is he talking about the objects in
Sol's garage?

"Not only natural objects," Abel Moore goes on. "Don't dismiss me out of hand! Don't be led into temptation! Think of the animist who believes each object stores its creator's or its user's energy, whoever loved or hated it. He recognizes life in drums, in knives, in seashells. He brings a dish of milk to feed the cowbell."

The big man frowns and shades his eyes with his hand as if there's too much light in the room. "Sometimes I'm greedy. I try for too much and that's a mistake. I look to where I want the ball to go, not at the ball. And it's imperative to keep your eye on the ball. When my concentration's pure, when I'm not too greedy, then I enter a sphere where ordinary rules don't apply. A sphere in which if you wash the knife that wounded you, the wound will be cleansed. It's beautiful in there! In there, I'm like a geologist reading rocks, except I read objects. In there, I'm the farmer feeding the cowbell."

He goes on and on. Nathan Sullivan's head lolls to one side and he falls half asleep.

Poppy sits quietly thinking about the streams of light she saw radiating from her fingertips. The odic force! One out of three can see it, and she's one of them!

ABEL MOORE POURS more water, sways a little to the left, squares his shoulders. "Now to demonstrate. What's necessary here is to stay inside myself; that's the whole thing: to stay inside your own perimeters! I need a few objects." The psychic looks around, then steps back and waits.

Poppy's job is to collect the objects. She snatches up a cardboard box from the back of the room and walks up and down the aisles with it, inviting audience members to drop in whatever they fish out of their purses or pockets: combs, pens, calculators, pillboxes.

Abel Moore watches her. "Put in what's meaningful to you, nothing expensive," he instructs mildly. Now comes the moment of truth. Now is the hour. Of course, he could deal in generalities (I see an unexpected journey, I see a letter bearing important financial news); this is the road most taken. So many walk down it and it's so crowded that it seems familiar, bound to lead to the promised land.

Poppy trots up to the stage with the box. Abel Moore steps forward, closes his eyes and gropes. What'll it be this time? A penknife that yesterday scraped a paint sample from an old molding? A pearl button that fell off a favorite blouse three years ago? Aha! He opens one eye. A pair of sunglasses, one lens slightly scratched, a gold-toned bridge to span the nose. Sunglasses to dim the landscape. He grasps the sunglasses delicately, as if he's afraid he'll drop them, or as if he's waiting for them to start vibrating like one of those buzzers the hostess gives you when you're waiting in a restaurant.

Out of nowhere (can this be possible?) he hears himself pronouncing: "The owner of these glasses recently visited a doctor because of a chip in his elbow." Now he's in for it. He's been specific; his "reading" will be verifiable. He said what he wasn't thinking, and now it's out there to be judged as he's to be judged. Lead me not into temptation, he counsels himself, but it's too late, he has to keep going, the expectant audience is imposing its will. He hesitates, then scurries down the path of least resistance: "The owner of these sunglasses has built his house against a mountain." No real harm there, but the sound of it is wrong and the sound never lies. It's too bad, but what can he do? He keeps marching the same road. "The world is won by those who let it go." One of those catch-all statements that no one's going to disagree with, one of those simple, subtle assertions that inches backwards towards the truth.

He gazes out at his audience and waves the sunglasses in the air, half expecting their owner to jump up and seize them, rescue them from his meticulous scrutiny, his interpretation. It would be easier to be a hypnotist (You won't remember your name when you wake up, and you won't want to smoke cigarettes either; your cigarettes will taste like pepper) instead of a psychometrist struggling to read objects, which much too often he fails miserably at.

At this moment Nathan Sullivan stands up and claims the sunglasses. "For the record," the old man says, "I visited the dentist recently for a chipped tooth, not a doctor about a chipped elbow. But I do have a summer home in the mountains—in the Blue Ridge—fifteen minutes from Bluemont."

Chipped tooth, chipped elbow, Abel Moore thinks; we shared the same road, but he was driving north and I was driving south. He glances at Opal to see how she's taking this mix-up; crossed signals come up more often than you'd think. How did he get into this predicament anyway? He'd meant to spend the last twenty years of his life fishing, not up on a stage performing like a trained bear.

Opal's face reveals nothing critical; it expresses interest and attention; she's not ready yet to give him a thumbs up or a thumbs down; the jury's still deliberating. Chipped tooth, chipped elbow. Something flawed—like the scratched sunglasses —but not broken. What does she want? You can't win em all! Lucky guess about the house in the mountains; flowers will fall whether he wills them to or not.

He puts down the sunglasses and returns to the cardboard box, fishes for another object to read, and this time draws forth a plain gold ring. Stuck in his thumb and pulled out a plum. A wedding band. Plainly, its owner not a believer in never removing this token, this promise of union.

He lifts the ring up, so all can see it, a plain gold band, too small for him, must be a woman's, but a blank eye this evening, shutting him out. "Who owns you?" he croons to it, "What do you want to tell me?" The gold circle gapes, tells him nothing, the silence is yelling at him, it's time for drastic strategy; what else can he do?

"Two years ago the owner of this ring had a face-lift," he improvises. That should do it; no one will claim the ring now; how could she? The owner, even if she denies the surgery, will worry she won't be believed, will sense that suspicions once hatched will forever linger. And now a leaden feeling suddenly comes over him, as if the ring's attached to a stone trap door that he can't pry open. Might not a few generalizations lighten the atmosphere? He searches his memory and comes up with: "If you always use a compass to draw a circle, you'll always remain a slave."

That should give her something to think about. He pauses, stares out at the sea of faces. It's quiet as the lake on Sunday morning; all eyes riveted on him, what else can he produce? Face-lift, think twice about using a compass to draw a circle ... how about, and he says it out loud, "It's a long lane that has no turning." She ought to be able to stitch together something from that cloth, not that, thanks to the face-lift, he'll ever know what it is.

He surveys the room in search of a guilty twitch, sees nothing, and is on the verge of returning the ring to the box when an old lady with upswept white hair stands up.

It's Edwina Poole.

"I had the face-lift three years ago, not two," she announces, turning her head slowly so everyone can catch a better look. "Why not look the age you feel instead of the age you are?"

She babbles on—a statement that compass or no compass, no real circles exist in nature, another statement that she's not a sheep and can provide witnesses who'll vouch for her uniqueness and rarity.

Abel Moore can't believe it. She not only underwent a face-lift, but she's standing up and admitting it in front of a hundred strangers, a performance Helen would never have considered. This old babe is one in ten thousand. Plus, he just made that up about the face-lift to hurry the evening along and now it turns out to be true. He glances at Opal to see if she can decipher this paradox (is even aware of it), but she's engrossed in what the old woman's saying.

A made-up face-lift that's turned out to be true. Forces at work that he neither understands nor necessarily even believes in. Not the first time he's spoken truer than he knows. Spoken beyond himself. He feels like he's met a flower blooming in the wrong season, a chrysanthemum inexplicably up in May. Or he's in a championship match, the ball is twice its normal size, there's no way he can miss his shot.

At last Edwina Poole sits down and eyes revert to the big man on stage who once more approaches the cardboard box. A look of sadness followed by a look of resolution crosses his face. He peers at the audience quizzically. Are they with him? This time he draws forth a black leather key chain with two dangling keys attached and something printed in gold letters on the black leather oval. He reaches for his glasses and reads out loud, "What does a fish know about the water in which it swims?" What indeed? Lots of people, himself included, prefer to live near water. He holds the key chain as if it were a remote control unit he plans to change the channel with.

For once Opal knows who the object belongs to—Geneva—because she gave it to her. At the Cosmos and Mind conference she attended a month ago, they distributed key chains as souvenirs. She took a green one for Poppy that asked, "Who is the third who walks always beside you?" And she took a red one for herself that stated, "Science as an interpreter of the mysteries of the universe is a dismal failure."

Abel Moore waits. He gives himself over to the life that inhabits the key chain, he believes in this life; what he's not sure of is that this life will choose to communicate with him. After all, why should it? He's waiting to hear (and the sound never lies), but he can't wait forever. He's on stage in a rented room, so he takes a deep breath, crosses his fingers, and falls back on his old standby: he says the first thing that darts into his head. "I see a lost book. It's slipped behind a filing cabinet." Not bad. Lots of people misplace books; he's done it dozens of times himself. In any case people read too much, depend too much on secondhand experience; better if more books were lost. A moment of silence and then he says, "A store of small strengths makes you strong." Another blanket statement. Let it cover this situation—whatever this situation turns out to be. One more prediction should do it; less than three seems skimpy. He waggles the keys as if they were a baby's rattle and meant to pacify. "Something about planting a tree," he says. "There's a desire to plant a tree." Safe enough. Who hasn't had thoughts of planting a tree? He's about to lay the keys down and call it quits when one more prediction happens. Before he can censor the thought that occurs to him, he blurts it out. "The key's owner will be fired from a job." The psychic hesitates a moment and adds, "This isn't necessarily bad."

Geneva stands and claims the key ring. "Hard to say," she stammers, her usual apologetic, diffident, awkward self. "As for the lost book, it could be yes; it could be no; I'll have to check when I get home. And the tree. The tree is interesting. I wrote a letter to the mayor about cutting back some dangerous branches on a tree in my neighborhood, but I didn't consider planting one. Being fired from my job is also off the mark. I don't have a job."

Abel Moore listens thoughtfully. Geneva Lamb, the girl who seems superimposed. He likes her; why couldn't his reading have been more accurate? Still, planting a tree, pruning a tree; there's a connection. Trees point to growth. Championing growth or worrying about it are similar concerns. He opens his mouth to explain, but Geneva begins to reflect out loud. "Maybe I should be planting a tree, not worrying about an overgrown one. Maybe I have to act myself and stop looking to the authorities. Maybe I'm too timid." Geneva scans the room as if she expects a discussion to erupt or at least a murmur of assent to arise. But the audience is still (figuratively) scratching its head, trying to make up its mind. Silence reigns.

Abel Moore dredges up a half smile, shrugs, steps back. He's done what he can; he would have liked to do better. "Fired from her job" seemed so clear; why is he never certain when his powers are switched on or off? He focuses once more on Opal, ready to follow her lead, her assessment of his performance. At last he catches her eye and she—wonder of wonders—smiles. It can't have been a total fiasco then (which has happened to him once or twice). He's defeated the odds and lobbed over his opponent's head.

Right about the house in the mountains, Opal thinks, right about the face-lift, close on the chipped elbow and on the tree. Not bad. It could have been worse. Much, much worse. She feels her anxiety of the last week drain away. Her worrying is past tense now; the present is all denouement and wrapping up. Not bad. Up on the stage, she warmly shakes the psychic's hand, reminds the crowd about the reception and to pick up any item they dropped in the box. Oh yes, it could have been much, much worse!

AT THE RECEPTION the guests sample miniature roast beef and turkey sandwiches, red and green grapes, jam-filled cookies. They sip soft drinks or wine from plastic glasses.

Opal drifts among the crowd, receiving compliments for her introduction. Gratifying to do a simple task well. Like those exercises of daily life they used to practice. *Pretend you're feeding fish in an aquarium. Make it convincing. What kind of fish are they? Don't give them too much. Do you like these fish or hate them? Pretend you're wallpapering a room. It's immaterial whether you've ever actually wallpapered a room. Believe that you're doing it now. Think of what you know about the art of covering up. Everyone's an expert at that!*

She munches a sandwich as she approaches Edwina Poole. "Facelift," she says. "I'd never have guessed."

"No?" Edwina's pleased. "I also study tai chi. It combats osteoporosis. The exercises cause you to sink into yourself. I'd never realized how important it is to do that. The Chinese perform these exercises at dawn in the parks."

Another old lady standing nearby says, "You know, all my life I lived with others, first with my parents, then with other students in the dorm, then with my husband. Last year, after fifty-two years, I became a widow. For the first time in my life I'm alone. It's very free. I don't have to clean or cook, I don't have to do anything. Very free!"

Angelica Fairfax extracts from her purse a newspaper article and thrusts it at Opal. "Here's the other article I promised. True story about a modern Rip Van Winkle. A modern Sleeping Beauty. At age thirty-three, this lady fell into a coma and didn't regain her faculties for seventeen years. She fell asleep in 1926 and rejoined the world in 1943. After she woke up, she became a full professor, but she'd missed the invention of ice cubes. She'd never ridden an escalator. She'd never heard of an electric blanket. She practically missed World War II. Never heard of Eleanor Roosevelt. When she celebrated her ninetieth birthday, she claimed she was only seventy-three."

Opal tucks the clipping into a pocket. "Thanks."

Angelica sighs. "I identify with this woman. Fighting back from nowhere. Having to reestablish herself. It's an experience African Americans can relate to." Angelica fans herself with a paper plate. "It's hot in here, don't you think?"

"It is a little warm," Opal agrees.

"Know what I mean?" Angelica asks. "Many segments of African history have vanished. Many famous people were black, but history books ignore it. Pushkin, the Russian writer, had a black ancestor. A black man invented the traffic light. An African American thought up the ironing board. There's a conspiracy to deny the significant role of the African in history, to whitewash culture."

Opal nods in agreement. No doubt Angelica's right. She doesn't know as much about African American history as she should. But she's curious about the subject at hand. "What did you think of Abel Moore?"

"Interesting gentleman. I've known many individuals with psychic powers."

"Of course!" The room's full of people who can make that statement.

Angelica frowns and elaborates. "Many people of African origin possess psychic powers. Our alienation from society has strengthened our insight. It's Emerson's law of compensation: remove one thing and another springs up to replace it."

"I believe that."

"My god, it's hot in here," Angelica complains, fluttering the paper-plate fan. "In our community, we understand the remote roads of the spirit. We subscribe to off-beat intellectual theories, and why shouldn't we? Hasn't the mainstream bashed us for centuries? Haven't the scientists and the economists and the sociologists flattened us with their standard appraisals? They've pinned us wriggling to the wall, just as T.S. Eliot says. But we've managed. We said one thing and thought another; we pretended to agree, but continued believing otherwise. That once there were four moons. That lions fell from one of them. That events of earth are in sympathetic relationship with celestial things. That the stars are fighting on the side of the just."

"Any thoughts about pre-Columbian African influences in the new world?" Opal asks.

Angelica doesn't miss a beat. "Nubian Egyptians came to the Americas a thousand years B.C. and influenced the Olmec culture of Mexico. If you don't believe me, look at the artifacts of both cultures. They both used the double crown; in both cultures purple symbolized sacred and royal life; both cultures featured ceremonial boats, artificial beards, feathered fans, ritual umbrellas."

"Think there's an article there for the *Zoetic Review?*" Opal murmurs.

Angelica smiles, crushes her paper-plate fan, drops it in a trash container, and promises to write the article.

Besides those seeking Abel Moore's autograph, the group around him want to pick his brain, size up his reactions. The man with the red eyes wants to know if the psychometrist believes the human race is mutating towards a higher or a lower state. The woman in white stockings and sandals volunteers, "My mother once dreamed of a skull and crossbones on a medicine bottle, and two days later my brother poisoned himself!"

"Sorry to hear about your brother." Abel Moore thrusts his hands deep into his pockets. What prompts people to make such startling revelations? Only last week a young man confessed he'd accidentally run over a child.

Dionne Inglenook interrupts. Does he have an opinion about gem elixirs?

Abel Moore does not.

Mabel Sullivan interjects a different request. Would he be available for an ESP conference that the Smithsonian has organized for July? She knows it's short notice, but the leader of a workshop on prosperity meditation cancelled at the last minute.

Abel Moore promises to check his schedule.

Mona Friendly flutters up in her sea-foam-colored dress. "Cayce insisted there's one basic energy and all specific kinds—gravity, electromagnetism, atomic, etc.—are simply variations of it."

Later, Abel Moore approaches the table where Poppy's tending the magazines.

"Poppy Greengold," she says. And immediately, "I have a question."

"Fire away." Will he be able to answer it? Probably not. It seems to be his fate this evening. But he'll try.

"Do you think there's anything to the theory that the further back on the head the ear is, the greater the intellect?" This question is one of ten that Poppy scribbled on a sheet of paper earlier that morning.

"Position of the ear?" Abel Moore is startled. Where do people dig up such off-the-wall questions? That woman at the lecture last week— her hair like a swarm of bees—who asked if time had gravity. How should he know? He's not a physicist. To Poppy he gives the same response he gave her. "No idea."

Poppy plunges on with question two. "What do you think about disappearing stars?"

Again Abel Moore pleads ignorance.

But Poppy refuses to be daunted. "My mother always dreamed of seeing Haley's Comet. It only appears every seventy-three years and its last sighting was in 1986. She wanted to travel to an observatory to see it, but my father convinced her not to go. He called her a fool. She tried to catch a glimpse of it from our backyard, but that didn't work. The next year my father died, and that one incident is all she seems to remember about her marriage."

"Curious." What makes some men so bull-headed? Insecurity? Blocked chi? He wouldn't have tried to stop Helen. And he wouldn't have succeeded if he had.

"Disappearing stars made me think of it."

Abel Moore picks up the *Zoetic Review* and pages through until he finds his article. Although the article's been out for six months, he still enjoys seeing his name in print. He never expected to be an author. He closes the magazine but keeps his finger on the page where his article begins. "I hoped to retire to a shack by the lake. Spend my days fishing. Drive to the hardware store in town for bloodworms and fish hooks."

He half smiles at the thought. His personal revelation for hers. Helpful that she's a stranger because sometimes it's easier to talk to strangers. With strangers it's only words. He extracts his finger and returns the magazine to the stack. "And you? What's your Haley's Comet?"

"I don't know. I'm trying to figure it out. In the meantime, I volunteer at the Society. And I read a lot."

"What do you read?"

"Right now I'm reading about Mother Hutton. She was a biologist who discovered digitalis, although a man got the credit."

"Never heard of her."

"Thousands of women have made major contributions and no one's ever heard of them," Poppy says a little bitterly. "A woman invented Scotchgarding. A woman invented Liquid Paper."

"Amazing." He tugs at his tie. What can he say about thousands of unrecognized women? No doubt she's right. But what can he do about it? She sounds like Deb. Idealistic.

"So many women spent their lives in prison," Poppy says.

"Do you think they saw it that way?"

"Some did." Then, trying to keep the conversation even, "Who do you read?"

"Wilhelm Reich."

"Should I know him?" It's never-ending the list of authors she should read. There are probably as many unread books as there are unknown women. She'll never catch up. She glances at the big man opposite her who's looking a little melancholy, and feels a sudden rush of affection for him. A man who's found lost money and lost children. She feels an affinity with him. Like her, he's been chosen.

Sensing her scrutiny, the psychic smiles. She's forgiven him for not being able to answer her unanswerable questions. A pleasant girl. Pretty too. An unexpected serious side to her. Obscure women. Disappearing stars. Any pattern here?

"I'm not sure school's for me." Poppy makes this statement matter-of-factly, as if Abel Moore's been following the argument she's had with herself the last few months. "I get bored. My mind won't focus."

"That happens to everybody."

"Does it?"

"It does." What would it be like to be twenty-three? Younger than Deb! Her life before her! If he were that age, would he make the same choices? Knowing what he knows now? Still end up selling auto glass? Probably, but who knows?

"I have a two-year-old son." Poppy isn't sure why, but she wants Abel Moore to know this.

"His name?"

"Metro." And Poppy, twisting her garnet ring around and around her finger, tells him about the derailed Metroliner, about Vic, about her rescue at Chadwick's.

"Good lord!" Abel Moore takes a handkerchief from his pocket and mops his face. Such a complicated history! A vanished lover, a child, a sense of destiny! And only twenty-three! How different from Deb who ever since childhood has known exactly what she was doing. An A student in high school, Dean's list in college, now a public service lawyer. Always busy. So far, too busy to start a family.

"One more thing," Poppy says.

"I'm all ears."

Poppy smoothes back her hair. "The way I see it, this universal force you're talking about is no more than the Goddess. She who is the author of all being, she who infuses all creation with the vital blood of life."

Again, Abel Moore fiddles with his tie. Why does he always feel two steps behind this young woman? Is it her youth that gives her statements such edge? "The vital blood of life?" Where does a phrase like that come from? Although given to sweeping statements himself, he's suspicious when others make them.

"She's had a thousand names," Poppy goes on.

"A thousand names?"

"Aurora, Demeter, Eve, Mother Goose."

That's four, not a thousand, Abel Moore thinks but does not say.

"She's called Aphrodite, Kali, Medea, Artemis, Athene, Neith, Medusa, Isis, Delilah, Kore—"

"You've done a lot of reading on this subject." Good lord. What has he stumbled into?

"I have." Suddenly, Poppy thrusts her pocketbook at Abel Moore. "Hold this a minute for me, would you? I'll get you some wine."

"No need," he protests, but she's already gone, so he stands clutching her slim little pocketbook.

An impression forms.

Of vegetal spirits in a garden and Poppy among them.

When Poppy returns, he says, "I saw you in a garden with vegetal spirits."

She hands him a glass of red wine. "Vegetal spirits! What are vegetal spirits? I live in an apartment. I have a geranium, an African violet, and a spider plant."

He thanks her for the wine. The abruptness of the young. How like Deb she is. How certain she's figured everything out. Best to change the subject. "How are sales going?"

Poppy consults a little notebook. "Thirty copies of the magazine."

"Wonderful!"

"All because of your article!"

At this moment, Abel Moore is cornered and carried off by two admirers who want to know his opinion about acrylic crystal balls.

Later, Abel Moore encounters Geneva who has, he's noticed, spent most of the evening talking to a man with greying hair.

"I have a question," she says.

Abel Moore tells her to shoot.

She asks about Yeats' gyres. The spinning cones that whirl between subjectivity and objectivity. And about Yeats' Four Faculties of the Soul. Will and Mask, Creative Mind and Body of Fate. Can he tie these concepts into his universal force theory?

"Unsure," he admits. "I need to study Yeats. But I'll be coming back for a program at the Smithsonian in July, and maybe we could have lunch and discuss it then."

The evening winds down. Opal stands alone, overlooking the room where people are saying good-bye and the hotel staff are scooping up empty plastic cups and discarded paper plates. Depleted trays of food are carried off, chairs folded and stacked against a wall. The evening is almost over; in a few minutes she'll be able to be herself again. It will be a tremendous relief to retreat to a more private state. A state that tangles her concern with dry lips with her concern to find out more about morphic fields. A state that juxtaposes "grape juice cures cancer" with the concept of the universal mind as a star with billions of points.

But first things first. She takes a deep breath, approaches Moore, and hands him an envelope containing the thousand-dollar check.

"Thank you," he says.

"Thank *you*."

Poppy comes up to say good-bye.

"Vegetal spirits," Poppy says. "Can I write you?"

"I'd be happy if you would."

After Poppy leaves, Opal asks, "Does the memory of a bone in the throat connect with the theory of morphic fields?"

"Bone in the throat? Dr. Westcot's the expert here. As I understand it, each system has a morphic field. Each onion, for example, has its own field. And the fields communicate by a kind of resonance."

"I see." Not that she does.

"It's a question of keeping your eye on the ball. My approach is a little different. Think about spirit in matter … the chi inside a thing."

"Your 'readings' went well."

"No law against being lucky. Even a blind pig sometimes finds a truffle. The way I see it, things are the ambassadors of a silent world. They're not cluttered with quirks, the way people are. The common belief is that matter is simply matter. Inert. Unfeeling. But I believe things are pure. That they're misunderstood. I believe that salt can sing. That a water jug contains the seven seas."

Opal deliberates half a second before asking, "Would you write an article for us on the inner life of objects?"

"Possible," the psychic says. "I'll stay in touch. I'll be in town in July."

Dr. Westcot appears at the psychic's elbow to escort him home.

Although tired, Abel Moore doesn't want the evening to end. Good to be appreciated. To be Man of the Hour. Still, a long time since he danced till dawn. He clasps Opal's hand, then follows Dr. Westcot.

In the car, the envelope with the check inside vibrates in his hand. Abel Moore closes his eyes and allows his thoughts to wander. As they unravel, he sees Opal rambling among a cluster of discarded chairs. A doorless, upended refrigerator stands on her right. She's dressed in jeans and looking for something. Looking for what? But he never sees what it is, because suddenly a cat darts into the street and Dr. Westcot abruptly brakes. Abel Moore lurches forward, but his seatbelt prevents injury.

"Sorry," Dr. Westcot says.

"No problem." Jolted back into the present, Abel Moore's vision of Opal gradually dissipates as he gives himself to a discussion of mystic cats.

AT HOME OPAL kneels, trying to remove a coffee stain from the beige carpet in her study. It's after midnight. What was she thinking of when she knocked over that cold half cup? Coffee's the worst stain; she should have been more careful; she should have been drinking green tea.

She blots the excess with a wad of paper towels, foams carpet cleaner onto the spot, waits a few minutes, blots again. *Out damned spot,* but it's already obvious she's going to have the same problem the Scottish queen had: this spot's not going to disappear easily. What was that acting exercise? *Pretend you're bailing water from a leaking boat. Remember to strip away whatever's nonessential.*

Bailing water from a leaking boat. The story of her life. This stain's just one example. She's embarked on a Sisyphean task: she's going to work hard, she's not going to succeed.

In spite of this conviction, she sprays again, blots again. *Strip away whatever's nonessential.* Excellent advice. If only she could follow it. Mr. Koldaro was emphasizing the need for clean, economical gestures, but the admonition could stand as a general motto. Like the inspirational sayings tacked around Sol's studio. This could be hers. Cut out what's extraneous. Don't allow yourself to be distracted. Simplify. Keep focused.

Not easy for someone who studied being a chameleon. Who aspired to be an actress. Who posed as a mannequin in a store window. Who waddled like an eggplant. Who practiced collapsing like a cracked eagle's egg.

Try Windex? Since the carpet cleaner seems to be having little effect. She finds the blue liquid, sprays it onto the carpet, rubs with a sponge. The pile of the carpet lathers up; it looks like the spot's disappearing, but is it? Maddening. It's coffee she's spilled, not ink, not paint. Some product's bound to take it out. The question is, which one?

Still, a stain on the carpet's not the end of the world. She can reposition the furniture so a table covers the discolored area. Replace the carpet.

She sits back.

Fortunately, she can still sit on the floor.

Those long ago parties where she spent the evening sitting on the floor pretzeled into a half lotus, listening to music.

Smoking.

She'd smoked the pot Zach brought her and it helped. She'd felt better. Her head opened up; the chemo-induced nausea subsided, became muted. Before that, thirty years since she smoked. She'd quit in her twenties, opting for health and a clear head. It was time to put away her childhood and grow up. Strip away the nonessential.

The pot was nonessential, so she let it go.

What else has she dropped?

Her desire to become an actress. Her desire to be center stage. Enough to be a bit player.

Her conviction that clothes, once removed from the dryer, require folding.

She no longer insists that everything make sense. She'll consider "the soul of objects" tomorrow.

She's practically given up alcohol.

She hasn't painted her fingernails in twenty years.

She's given away most of her college texts.

Abandoned the ideal of symmetry.

Stopped dying her hair.

Her mother and sister. She hasn't given them up; she talks to them frequently but no longer knows the details of their lives. They've fallen away from her.

Things don't fall apart (as Geneva keeps quoting); they fall away.

Her life's shrinking. Literally, she's an inch shorter than ten years ago. She's simplified. And left herself with what? A husband who's probably asleep on the sofa. A son whose forces seem scattered. A job she has questions about. A handful of vitamins she swallows every day. An exercise regime she too often skips. The feeling that her life consists of bailing water from a leaking boat.

Rosalie considers her a lightweight. Is it her fault if she finds accounts of odd events fascinating? Pyramids discovered in Russia. Rocks, stolen from the Petrified Forest, which had to be returned after they brought bad luck to their owners. The unearthing of a Neanderthal-era bone flute with four holes. She doesn't automatically believe such accounts. She strives to keep an open mind.

Would Rosalie like her better if she read the *Wall Street Journal?*

Rosalie likes her well enough.

Since she's on the floor, she might as well exercise. Important to breathe. To inhale the universe.

She sits in a half lotus, straightens her back, slowly exhales. Then breathes in and holds the caught breath. Counts to four. Slowly releases it. Repeats the sequence. Eight times she inhales the universe and blows it out again.

The energy's flowing. The chi's flowing. It's after midnight, but better late in the day than not at all. Now to think back to some victorious moment in her life. Translate the feeling of that time into the present. Not think back, but see back. See that time. No intellect required. Or allowed. She closes her eyes, waits for an image to form. And one does. It's of herself, nine years old, playing with other kids in her backyard.

There's a Russian olive tree and a crepe myrtle. There's a blue gazing globe. What they're playing is a game called Swing the Statue. Whoever's "it" swings the other players around and around, then releases them and watches as they tangle in heaps on the grass. Everyone holds their breath, everyone's afraid to move; they have to pretend they're statues. It's twilight, cicadas are singing; a soft, endless summer evening.

The point of the game's to see how long you can stay in the position you've landed in. How long can you be a statue. How long before you start to giggle or squirm or your leg starts to itch and you have to scratch it. The first one to move loses and has to swing the other players. But losing's no worse than not losing. Swinging the others, being swung, both are equally good.

The game goes on until it's dark. But the coming of night doesn't matter. Night's only a temporary interruption. Summer will go on forever. Tomorrow they'll play again. And the next day.

Opal reaches out and touches the carpet, touches the damp circle, which surrounds the spot that has lightened but not disappeared. She'll let the spot thoroughly dry and tomorrow try something else.

DOWNSTAIRS, SOL CHANGES into more comfortable clothes and pulls on his slippers. He feels like hell. Stuffed-up nose, scratchy throat, ringing ears. A headache. He rummages in the garage until he finds an old vaporizer that no one's touched for years, which he scrubs carefully before filling. The vaporizer is aqua and squat. Like an overgrown toad. Now he sits on the mustard-colored sofa in his studio and waits for the steam to come and unclog him. Should he take two aspirin? An antibiotic? He doesn't have an antibiotic. Tomorrow he'll fill that prescription.

As he waits for the steam, he imagines he's entering his second childhood. Once, at about age seven, after his father set up a vaporizer and showed him how to make a tent out of the bedclothes, Sol spent the day huddled under the sheets, inhaling the steam, drawing it deeper and deeper into his lungs.

Steam's good for you, said his father, adjusting the sheets. *It will clear out your system.* According to his father, that's what he needed. Maybe that's what he still needs. But now it's more than germs. Now every stale idea, every hesitation needs to be steam-blasted and sweated out.

How has he become so clogged? So obsessed with the past, so caught in a tangled present. So blocked. The opposite of his father who allowed nothing to stand in his way. Who managed to skirt every barricade. A man on a mission and in a hurry to complete it. Didn't he drive like a madman, only now and then checking the rearview mirror for cops? Didn't he furiously invent a life for himself? Didn't he, a watchmaker, force time to do his bidding? Zach also doesn't waste time worrying. Like his grandfather, he charges ahead, trusting the future. Didn't he buy his car without comparing prices? Isn't he thousands of dollars in debt? Isn't he off to Boulder charging his ticket, whatever he needs? Nothing impedes him. He ignores every snag. He hovers like an archangel, tall, beautiful, slightly fierce. He soars above every difficulty. He's optimistic and lighthearted, banks on his glittering smile, his angelic sweetness.

Upstairs he hears Opal. She thinks he's a hypochondriac and will laugh at his steam kettle, the sweater he's pulled on (you're wearing a sweater in the middle of May!), his sheepskin slippers.

Tonight he'll never sleep; he's too excited, his head's spinning. What did Abel Moore say? *The soul of objects.*

He pulls a book from the shelf and pages through it. Then another one. Then another. Three books later, he still hasn't found what he's looking for, a quote he once read. If he could find it, he'd tack it on the wall. He returns to the sofa and inhales deeply from the steam kettle. The vapor makes the studio slightly mysterious, as if he's viewing it from up in the clouds. Was it Kandinsky? *Everything quivers. Even a white trouser button in the sleet is beautiful.* Something like that. Same philosophy as Abel Moore. Everything has a secret soul.

The steam's pouring out now, turning the studio into strips of gauze, into sheets of swaying muslin. It's filling his lungs like smoke, reaching deep inside him, into his nose, his throat, his chest. Loosening his spirit (just a little), giving it a push, encouraging it to move around, to stretch, to venture forth.

The studio's so fogged up, his paintings almost vanish. Insects in a jar. Never mind, his sketchbook brims with ideas for paintings. A bear with a wound in its side that looks like a clock, a dog with eyes pulled shut like window shades, a snake curled around a rock of frozen blood.

A rock of frozen blood.

An object awakens our love … because it seems to be the bearer of powers that are greater than itself. This quote (Bazine?) is tacked up over his worktable.

An object, any object. Even the Golem, the man made from mud by a fourteenth-century rabbi. If everything has a soul, wouldn't this arti-ficial man have one? As a trouser button has one, an umbrella stand has one, a grain of sand has one.

A cowbell has one and requires a dish of milk.

He checks the time. The vaporizer's been pouring out steam for fif-teen minutes. This can't be good for his paintings. He hauls himself up and disconnects the device; its steamy trail sputters, then vanishes like a ghost. In a minute the air is clear, the studio regains focus.

He sees it with fresh eyes.

You should clean this place up, he knows Opal thinks, but does not say. She says it about the garage, where he stores old bottles and maga-zines and tools and dozens of other useless—in Opal's view—items, but she keeps her lip buttoned about the studio. Still, he knows what she thinks. You don't stay married to a woman for thirty-two years without knowing what she thinks.

But the studio is his space and he likes its clutter, its shelves chockablock with books and brushes, tubes of paints, solvents, bottles, rags, knives. Slogans across the walls. The black metal file containing reports by the detective who investigated his father.

Opal believes in magic. She equates inside to outside, a cluttered garage and studio to a cluttered spirit. Maybe she's right. But she fails to recognize that artifacts have secret souls. That they're alive. The trick is knowing how to approach them. His father, another magical thinker, plugged in the vaporizer to clear out his system, unfetter his spirit. Opal looks like his father. The eyes are the same brown and the webbing of tiny lines when she smiles is the same. There's also resemblance in the way her hair is turning grey, as his did, like a grainy pebble.

Believers in magic. There's her pad and pencil next to his painting. She's expecting a half-finished figure to speak to her. Write to her. Write with what? No use pointing out that his figure, an insect, has wings, not hands, so even if she wanted to write, she couldn't.

Wings. Hands. It's the same to Opal. She believes in phone calls from the dead, so why not letters from a winged insect. A painted winged insect.

Anything's possible.

Anything can make sense. The belief of Botticelli (pinned up over his work table): *If you throw a paint-soaked sponge at a wall, in the splashes it makes you will see heads, animals, landscapes.*

He reaches over and turns on the radio. Very softly, so as not to disturb Opal.

He *is* feeling better. That steam has opened him up, and he takes a deep breath to test his perception. Nasal passages open, throat less raw, ears no longer ringing. He stretches, goes over to examine his painting in progress, opens a window and lets the warm night air brush against him, gentle as a bird's wing. There's a sweet smell in the air that he knows but can't identify. A moth knocks up against the screen, trying to get in, drawn by the overhead light. He's here in his studio, a sixty-year-old man, but he could be seven again, awake at night and listening. He's always been listening, and he's still listening. He's always been waiting, and he's still waiting.

He picks up a brush. One day he might stuff this painting in a tube and shove it in a corner. But for the moment, it's facing him on the easel, and he's clutching a paintbrush as if it were a sword. A sword to beat back the waves that threaten to annihilate him. Who was that Roman emperor who attacked the sea? He squints to recapture the vision that once he imagined, but now the shapes are not well balanced, the line of the jar is too heavy, the mass of leaves at the bottom not in proportion. A balance in his own mind has shattered, and now the shapes of the three figures are wrong; the forces they represent have lost tension; it's too literal, there should be more blurring, more super-imposition, the design is too heavy, the parts are not supporting the whole, the concept of wholeness. Does that mean he has to start over, try again to get back to that original concept, or will simply looking lead him back ... but back to what? He applies a daub of umber and a shadow emerges. He holds it in his mind, willing it not to escape, but the line of the jar is still too definite; it interrupts his vision, yet he hangs on to it, tries to fix it. He alters the shape of the third figure a little, the one he calls Emilia, yes, it's better with this line blurred, that one half painted over.

Four hours later he wanders into the kitchen where he finds an ice cream bar in the freezer, which he eats before collapsing onto the mustard-colored sofa and falling asleep.

GENEVA WALKS ON her treadmill, a stupid occupation she'd be the first to admit, but where else can she walk at midnight on a Saturday in Washington, D.C.? She takes brisk, forceful steps; she can feel her heart beating, which means her adrenalin is flowing, her blood is circulating. She'll walk for fifteen minutes, a skimpy workout, but fifteen minutes is her limit. Even with the TV on, which it isn't now, Geneva gets bored. Walking fast and getting nowhere doesn't match her idea of interesting.

She's stripped off her green silk dress and is walking in her bra and underpants. She's barefooted too—bored but unrestricted. Her green dress is draped over the back of a kitchen chair, on its way to the closet. *Left! Right! Left! Right! Left my wife and forty-nine kids in a starving condition without any gingerbread. Did I do Right? Right? Right by my country, by George, by Jingo, did I do Right?*

She turns the brisk walk into a march, as she once did at Camp Belle Haven twenty years ago. It's one of two things she remembers from camp, the other her role as the Moon in a modern dance program, a part that required her to wander the stage draped in a sheet, arms circled above her head.

She glances at her watch. Five more minutes. Going through the motions, it's the story of her life. Wasting time on what she doesn't believe in. She's always done it. All those languages she studied in school: French, Spanish, Latin, German, Old English, Middle English. She forgot everything the day the classes ended. What was the point? Obstacles to be overcome. She overcame them, but so what?

She's walking on the treadmill tonight because she's on pins and needles. Afraid she won't sleep. If she exercises, maybe she'll tire herself out and be able to drop off. Unless it works the other way, and exercise will only further stimulate her.

She's in a stew because, one, Abel Moore invited her to lunch. He's too old, sixty if he's a day, but a date's a date. And he's tall, which too many men are not, and interesting—a hundred people paid money to hear him speak. Of course, lunch doesn't mean anything, it's just the meal eaten at noon, and some conversation about Yeats, which she should be able to manage, unless she's forgotten it all by then.

Left! Right! Left! Right! The window pane is shattered where the rock came through, and the room feels chilly. Geneva likes the starkness of the room, the lack of furniture. Sofas and chairs are overrated—chains, if you think about it. Not having furniture keeps you more alert, more on your toes—literally, since there's nothing to sit on.

Her feet are starting to sweat. She should wear shoes on the treadmill but prefers going barefoot. She likes the sensation of different surfaces beneath her feet. *How can foot feel, being shod?* Hopkins asks, and she agrees. Her feet look better without shoes; they provide a proportionate base for her height. Too often, her shoes don't even look like shoes, they look like boats or like baked potatoes. She'd give a tooth for a size seven shoe. While she's making wishes, she wouldn't mind being four inches shorter. She'd like to be five-seven and wear a size seven shoe. Dream on, my girl, she tells herself. However, there are advantages to her size. She can see in crowds, she can eat more than a bagel for lunch, she is a substantial person.

She walks steadily on the treadmill.

Reason two for her confusion is George Bluestone. The mystery man from the third floor. Who'd have guessed he'd show up at the lecture? Who'd have guessed he'd single her out afterwards?

"Excuse me," he said. "You work downstairs, don't you?" Then he announced, "George Bluestone," and stuck out his hand.

She took it. "Geneva Lamb," she replied, her voice firm. He'd noticed her! Suddenly she saw she'd entered a foreign country with eccentric customs. Confusing yet exciting! How should she act? What should she say? Would she be understood?

His hand was smooth and slightly warm, a nice hand. He offered to get her—to get them—some wine, and she watched him thread through the crowd. Most of her sightings of him had been at a distance; he looked different up close. Tall. Two tall men in one night—what was happening to the world?—and thin, a narrow face. Grey eyes behind round, steel-framed glasses, which made him resemble a Russian intellectual of the thirties. His hair, greying above his ears, was a little shaggy, and this too made him look Eastern European. Unless it was just a bad haircut. Nevertheless, distinguished-looking. Boyish.

"Odd lecture," he said when he reappeared with the wine. "Odic force. Bio Energy. All those old ideas."

"Old ideas?"

"They've been floating around for more than a hundred years. Mesmer discovered animal magnetism around 1760. Reichenbach experimented with crystals in the mid-1800s."

Geneva took a nervous swallow of wine. She stared at George Bluestone's left ear as if she were undergoing an eye exam. She couldn't remember any historical dates except 1066—Norman Conquest—and 1875—the year Yeats was born.

"Reichenbach published his book in 1845. I'm writing a book on Arthur Conan Doyle. The Sherlock Holmes guy. He was fascinated by the occult."

Geneva told him she'd written a dissertation on Yeats, also fascinated by the occult.

"I'd like to read it."

She almost dropped her plastic wineglass. No one had ever expressed interest in reading her dissertation before. Surely this *was* a foreign country!

George Bluestone smiled. A nice smile, slightly irreverent. He swished his wine like a connoisseur. "A few people believe Doyle was Jack the Ripper. Based on circumstantial evidence."

"Jack the Ripper!" An unexpected turn in the conversation. First, Mesmer and Reichenbach, then asking to read her dissertation, now Jack the Ripper!

George Bluestone's grey eyes behind his steel-framed glasses lit up. Obviously, he'd introduced a subject close to his heart. "I don't believe it, but you never know."

"You never do." Geneva switched her glass from one hand to the other.

"One evening we might discuss it over dinner. You could loan me a copy of your dissertation. If you would."

"I would," she said. Dinner with George Bluestone! She'd have to read up on Doyle. At least a decade since she'd opened a Sherlock Holmes story. Wasn't there one about a snake that slithered out of an air vent and attacked its victim?

She checks her watch. Fifteen minutes of fast walking. She turns the machine off and steps down. Sweat films her body, so she must be doing something right. George Bluestone asked for, and she gave him, her telephone number. Lunch with Abel Moore! Dinner with George Bluestone! In a way, she's already eaten a meal with George. Lunch that day she followed him.

She towels herself off, peels off her underwear, pulls on a blue shorty nightgown that's ten years old. She brushes her hair, but quits after twenty-five strokes—too boring—washes her face, slathers on moisturizing cream. Jack the Ripper. Would someone express interest in this character because he has similar inclinations? She shudders. What does she know about George Bluestone? Not much. He rents the office upstairs from the Zoetic Society office. He wants to read her dissertation. He claims he's writing a book.

Which reminds her. The book behind the filing cabinet. She checks, and (wonder of wonders!) Abel Moore was right, there is a book! She fishes it out. *The Collected Poems of Theodore Roethke*. Due at the library eight months ago.

On an impulse, she closes her eyes, opens the volume at random, and points. Her finger hits a verse from "Memory": *A doe drinks by a stream / A doe and its fawn. / When I follow after them, / The grass changes to stone.*

WHEN SHE FALLS asleep, she dreams about the deer. She chases them through a forest, but small trees and low-hanging branches block her, and she can't keep up. She slows to a walk, and now she's on a path, but all around the vegetation is dried and shrivelled, trees leafless, spears of grass brown, bushes dry and broken. She's never seen such an arid place. The stream where the deer were drinking has disappeared. And now the path's so hot and dusty, she can almost smell it. A smell of heat. Suddenly she awakes, but the acrid smell remains. Not unusual; dreams often meld into the non-dream world, engendering that blurred state between sleep and waking. She sits up, fully awake now, yet the air still smells sharp and thick.

She blunders out of bed and gropes for the light switch, but flipping it produces no result. Perfect time for a bulb to burn out or a fuse to blow or whatever it is. She sniffs again. It smells like smoke. Smoke! Not dust, not brown dryness. She's no longer dreaming, she's not in a forest, the smoke is real.

The house is on fire!

Her house is burning, smoke pouring under the door! Her eyes are adjusting to the dark, even though they're tearing; she sees the smoke and her head is starting to pound.

Why no warning from the smoke alarm?

Move it, Geneva. Don't just stand there. She gropes towards the closet, grabs tennis shoes and an old trenchcoat, pulls them on. The smoke is thicker now, her head is exploding, the smoke is invading her nose, her throat, her chest. She can't breathe. In the distance, sirens shrill.

Pull yourself together, girl. There's a solution to this problem. A way out. Not the door. An inferno lies beyond the door. The window?

She fumbles at the window. It rattles a little but doesn't open. Stuck. Like all the windows in this damn cottage, except the broken one in the living room. She rams a shoulder at the panes of glass; there's a dull, thudding sound, but nothing gives. The impact almost takes her breath away.

A rhyme begins in her head: *Lady bug, Lady bug fly away home. Your house is on fire ...*

Her house is on fire! An orange glow lightens the night sky beyond the sealed window, the wail of sirens grows louder.

Now is the time. Otherwise she's charred bones. She slams into the window again, aiming with her other shoulder. Nothing. She grabs Roetkhe's *Collected Poems* and whacks at the glass panes. Nothing. If only she had a chair! She's been too cavalier about furniture. If she lives to tell the tale, she'll have a chair in her next bedroom. Also a heavy lamp on an end table.

She almost blacks out but grabs onto the side of the bed to steady herself. She's trembling, stiff, can't breathe, the smoke is thickening. She's got to get out. She lurches back to the window, she's got to smash it, it's the only way, she's got to get out.

She pounds the window, then kicks it until finally a crack zigzags across a pane. Again she kicks, and this time the glass shatters. Thank god! She leans out and yells. She'll have to kick out a few more panes, then jump.

Suddenly matters are taken out of her hands. A thud against the side of the cottage as a firefighter puts up a ladder and then a cracking sound as his ax smashes what's left of the window. The glass falls away along with the wooden supporting partitions. He pulls her out and, half supporting her, helps her climb down.

After that, it's a blur. Flames shoot up and the roof collapses. Firefighters swarm, tramping in their boots and hosing the flames. Neighbors pour from their houses, many she's never seen before.

The same officer who brought her down the ladder leads her across the street to one of the parked trucks and invites her to sit down. He wraps her in a blanket, but she's still trembling. He wants to know if she needs medical attention, if she's going to collapse or erupt into hysteria.

"I'm fine," she insists. The officer has fair hair and fingernails bitten to the quick.

"Good idea to have a doctor look you over."

She doesn't need a doctor. She glances over to where, in spite of the streams of water pouring on it from thick hoses, her house is blazing away. Her house! What will happen to her books? Her papers? Her treadmill? Her typewriter? Nothing will be left.

The officer is preparing a report and hurls questions at her. What time did she go to bed? One A.M. Had she been smoking? No. Any appliances left on that she remembers? No. Is she the owner or a renter of the destroyed property? A renter. What is the name of the realty company that handles the house? She provides the name, and he makes a note. Is she sure she doesn't want to go to the hospital; it's routine to stay under observation for a couple of hours. She's fine. The last thing she needs is a trip to the hospital; hospitals are not for people with no health insurance.

She stares at her cottage. She asks the time, and the officer tells her: three A.M. Every single thing will be gone. Every single thing. Her head throbs and her side hurts when she shifts position.

A figure detaches from the crowd and approaches the truck. It's Brenda Lovejoy who offers her a place to stay.

"Is there room? What about your nephew?"

"Peter? He's gone. Called away unexpectedly."

Geneva hesitates. She sees Peter's blank-looking face, the noncommittal eyes behind clear plastic frames. Polite eyes, yet filled with disdain. A cat playing with a bird. Was she the bird? Nor has she had a chance to mention the rock to Brenda. She meant to, but hasn't.

"Plenty of room," Brenda offers. Her voice is pleasant and take-charge. Her grey hair circles her face like a cloud, and her eyes are kind.

Geneva goes. She signs off with the officer and, still draped in the blanket, traipses over to Brenda's. She can't sit in the fire truck all night. When the blaze is finally out, the firefighters cordon off the area and coil the hoses. The crowd disperses. The cottage no longer exists; it's a burnt-out shell with popped-out windows, its once unstable walls now charred and fallen. Once, in a class, someone asked: "Is an apple always an apple? What about when it starts to decay? To rot? It turns brown, then white and moldy, but it's still an apple, right? But at some point, as it breaks down, it stops being an apple. It becomes a heap of goo. The question is—when does the apple stop being an apple?" Good question. A matter of perspective. No doubt English lacks the vocabulary for certain subtle distinctions. Not like the Chinese bestiary, which provided multiple words for animal. One word for animals that belonged to the Emperor, another for animals that were lame, another for animals that were embalmed, another for animals that were drawn with a fine camel-hair brush, another for animals that behaved like mad things, another for animals that looked like flies from a distance.

Brenda offers orange tea, and Geneva settles on a stool at the kitchen counter. She adjusts the blanket around her shoulders; she feels like she's back in camp, draped in a sheet, about to impersonate the moon.

Next door, her house is rubble. An asteroid could have leveled it. Firemen will figure out how the blaze started in a day or two as airline investigators figure out what caused a crash. Faulty wiring? Something in the stove that ignited? Arson? Set by Peter? Not that she can prove it.

"Are you sure Peter's gone?" She wriggles her hands out from inside the blanket and cups her mug of fragrant tea.

"He left a note saying something came up." Brenda wipes the counter. "An odd young man. Friendly as a kid, but hard to talk to now. Withdrawn."

Geneva hugs herself. She feels chilled, though it's the middle of May. The trenchcoat and blanket aren't enough. She visualizes herself swimming in a heated pool, the warm water glassy around her, then tells her neighbor about the loud music, the phone calls, the call to the police, the broken window, the rock on her living room floor.

"What?" Brenda asks.

Geneva repeats the story.

"You don't think—" Brenda begins, but breaks off in mid-sentence because she doesn't want to think what she's thinking.

"I don't know."

"He said he was writing an opera about lost kingdoms under the sea. I thought it strange because he wasn't musically trained." Brenda offers this information, unsure of its relevance.

Geneva swallows her tea too quickly and coughs.

"He mentioned other grandiose plans," Brenda says, but doesn't elaborate.

When Geneva finishes her tea, Brenda makes up a bed in the guest room. Geneva tries to help, but she's all thumbs. Her cottage incinerated! All she has in the world are the clothes on her back. Her dissertation in ashes. Her address book. Her keychain with the inscription: *What do fish know about the water in which they swim?* She doesn't want to think about it.

So, for the second time that day—or night—Geneva goes to bed. This time she crawls under a rose-colored comforter in a room with fleur-de-lys wallpaper, a chest of drawers painted white, muslin curtains, a small armchair covered in flowery chintz.

The list of schools she applied to. Her notes for "The Esurient Kitty." The recipe for Katherine Hepburn's brownies. The blue topaz earrings her mother gave her when she graduated from college. Her green silk dress.

What will she do? What *do* people do when their houses burn down? When they lack walls, even unstable ones. When they've lost every book of poems they own, not even one left to poke a finger in for divination.

GENEVA SLEEPS UNTIL eleven A.M. When she wakes, it takes a moment before she remembers where she is—wallpaper with a fleur-de-lys pattern?—and the events of the previous night. She sits up and looks around. The sun is pouring through the muslin curtains, birds are singing.

Next door, her little cottage is no more.

It's unbelievable. Abel Moore's lecture. The fire. Peter's disappearance. Can these events be true? They must be, she couldn't have dreamed them up.

She climbs out of Brenda's bed. Her raincoat and the blanket provided by the fireman lie draped on the small armchair; her tennis shoes poke out from under the bed.

The house is quiet as a library. Brenda must be at work. She's lucky to have a job to go to … even if it's Sunday. Well, her time will come; it's got to. But until then … what is she supposed to do?

She pads barefoot—Hopkins would approve—into the bathroom and finds waiting for her a fresh towel, washcloth, grey sweatshirt, pants, housekey. A note reads: "Make yourself at home. I hope these fit. I work until four P.M., there're bagels in the fridge and coffee you can reheat in the microwave. I called the police and told them about Peter."

After a shower, having donned Brenda's sweats, she wipes the steamy mirror with her hand until her own blurred reflection stares back at her. The sleeves of the sweatshirt don't reach her wrists and the pants are too short. Still, she looks sporty. A woman who exercises. She could be heading out to run five laps. Her lost treadmill! She twists and turns, trying to view herself from every angle. Isn't there a movie where the characters, preparing for a journey to another galaxy, wore outfits like this? She looks prepared for a distant solar system.

She tugs at the sweatshirt and laces up her tennis shoes.

Her hair lies damp and flat for the moment, but soon enough it'll spring back to life and look like she stuck her finger in an electric outlet.

After a cup of reheated coffee, she treks next door. Not much to see: yellow tape cordons off the burned-out area. What was once her cottage is now a ruin. The neighborhood is silent. Her Victorian poetry text, so carefully annotated and cross-referenced. Photographs of her mother. Income tax records. Cancelled checks. Her combat boots.

Lucky to burn boots before embarking on a journey.

Her toothbrush.

It's Sunday, but she should be able to buy a toothbrush. Tomorrow she'll visit the bank for replacement checks, pick up new clothes. Maybe a sweatsuit in the right size. Since she never owned a credit card or an ATM card, she won't have to replace these items.

When she finds a job, she won't have much to move.

Back at Brenda's, she dials Opal (no answer) and Poppy (no answer). Could they be at the office? It's nearly noon. She wants to tell them about the fire. She wants their advice. Their support.

During her fifteen-minute walk to the office, she considers what she needs to do. Not necessary to file an insurance claim, because she doesn't have insurance. The cottage didn't belong to her. Only its contents. She walks as if in a trance. Her brain's half shut down.

She uses the emergency key, buried in a flowerpot, to let herself in. The office is empty. Where are they? A knock on the door interrupts her speculations, and she opens to George Bluestone, who invites her to lunch. Suddenly, she feels extremely hungry—when was the last time she ate?—and ten minutes later finds herself in the same deli she followed George Bluestone into four days ago. She hopes no one will mistake her for a blob of silly putty in this grey outfit. She hopes her hair doesn't resemble a puffball. She hopes the waitress won't recognize her.

To her relief, a man appears to take their order. George Bluestone orders a Swiss cheese sandwich, and she asks for the same. As soon as their platters arrive, she tells him about the fire. Her story produces an instant effect. George puts down his sandwich in mid-bite. "What?"

She repeats her story, omitting only her suspicions about Peter. Just because someone throws a rock through your window—

"Everything gone?"

"Everything." She eats a potato chip and licks her salty fingers. She's achieved celebrity status. She can see it in George Bluestone's eyes. His expression would be appropriate if she'd won an Olympic gold medal or starred in a made-for-TV movie.

George asks a lot of questions. Where is she staying? Does she need help finding another place? Would she be interested in his friend's efficiency that he's trying to sublet? What happened to her dissertation?

Does she need money? Would she like to borrow some? Any ideas about how the fire started?

She's touched. He's so forthright. So practical. So concerned.

She answers his questions, finally throwing in her suspicions about Peter. Why not? She's not accusing anyone, just reflecting.

As George Bluestone listens, his grey eyes behind his steel-framed glasses half close in concentration. "Revenge? It's possible. At least you weren't hurt."

A little embarrassed, she changes the subject to her job search, to which he says, "Hope you find something in the area."

"I'd like to see your friend's sublet," she says. She's eaten every crumb of her sandwich. Every potato chip. Also the wedge of lettuce and the pickle.

He invites her to dinner the following evening.

On the way back to Brenda's, she stops to buy a toothbrush and a notebook with the twenty dollars she borrowed from George. She feels uncommonly light. Her books are gone. Her papers. Her earthly possessions. She's like a snake who's shed her skin.

At Brenda's, she sits at the kitchen table and opens the notebook. She's re-listing possible words for "The Esurient Kitty" when the phone rings. It's a police officer with questions about the fire and the rock. He tells her the police aren't hopeful of establishing Peter's involvement, but they'll try to find him.

That evening, after she talks to Opal and Poppy, the phone rings again. The caller is the firefighter who helped her down the ladder. Her rescuer! He wants to know how she's doing, and asks if she'd like to drive up to Baltimore with him one evening and catch an Orioles game.

ON SUNDAY MORNING, Poppy walks along the C & O canal, which glints like foil in the eight A.M. sunlight. A twig crackles, a bird calls from a tree, but the sounds only emphasize the early morning silence. She could be a hundred miles from the city.

She heads west, towards Swain's Lock, walking on Mother Earth, drawing strength from the contact. Like Antaeus. In her blue baggy shorts, white oversized T-shirt, tennis shoes, hair in its customary pony-tail, she walks dreamily but steadily beside the trees and bushes that form a wall on her left, the narrow waterway on her right.

According to Russell, a series of interconnecting trails extend from the canal to Silver Spring. Crisscross the city. She doesn't know these routes, but maps must exist. If Russell has one, she could borrow it.

She can borrow a map from Russell, but she can't marry him. She's known it from the beginning, but buried the knowledge under practical considerations. He's good to Metro. Good to her. Her life's at an impasse and she needs to do something. All beside the point. The point is, she doesn't love him.

And Vic. She's still stuck on Vic. Vic the nomad.

A drumming stops her. High in a tree—what kind?—a woodpecker hops up and down, back and forth, pecking, looking for insects. His red crest jerks as he hops and thrums. This woodpecker's figured out his life; he wants insects, he pursues insects. Why can't she be like that? Decide what she wants and pursue it. She wants Vic, but doesn't even know what city he's living in.

She wants a career, but can't decide which one.

The woodpecker flies off, and she resumes her walk. She picks up her pace, and in a few minutes a line of sweat forms on the back of her neck, under her ponytail, which is switching back and forth. *Scottish girls weren't allowed to comb their hair at night when their brothers were at sea, for fear they'd raise a storm and sink the boats.* So she's read.

If Vic were at sea, would she unleash a storm and drown him? But a storm might wash him ashore. Where she'd be waiting? And then? Move twice a year with him? That's the problem.

So far, she's had the path to herself, not another person out. She reaches back, removes the scrunchie, and shakes her hair out. Let the storm come. Let Vic be swept away or swept back to her. Let what will be, be.

Soul not only in hair, but also, according to Abel Moore, in objects. Inanimate objects. *Old women in Devonshire after a death in the family tie up the flower pots with black crepe so the flowers won't droop and die.*

Flowerpots have souls.

Flowers.

Nothing like a walk. As a child, she summered at the Delaware shore, where she spent her afternoons walking in the fields among stiff grasses and wildflowers. She liked their delicate blooms, the sun on her legs, the salt air. In an earlier age, she might have been a nature worshipper, a druid or dryad.

There's still money in her account. Enough for a year, if she's frugal. Enough for more than a year, if she moves in with her mother, who'd like nothing better. But it's not what her mother wants, or what Russell wants. It's what she wants.

Which is?

A huge log lies off the path, and Poppy scrambles down and straddles it. What kind of tree? What felled it? She pokes its shredding bark and dislodges a colony of ants, which speed off as if they have a particular destination in mind. As if, like the woodpecker, they know exactly what they're doing.

She could follow her interests, take a class in botany or horticulture, learn to identify the trees. She could pick up a catalog at the university, a schedule of classes, an application form.

That should keep her busy tomorrow.

Look for a job. Whatever she decides, she'll need money.

She rakes her fingers through her loose hair. Let a storm come and wash away her fence-sitting life. If Vic shows up in the middle of the tempest, good; if not, other fish inhabit the sea. As do seahorses, star-fish, abalone, coral.

She resumes her dreamy walk. Farther along she notices etched in the grey bark of a large tree: *Isis lives*. The first *s* in Isis is half obliterated, but the message is unmistakable. *Isis lives*.

Isis who said, *I am Nature, the sovereign of the universe, the first of the heavenly gods and goddesses, the queen of the dead.*

With her fingers Poppy traces the name cut into the grey bark. *Isis lives*. Who says? Some witch? A local pagan group boasts a mailing list of five hundred in the Washington area. Witches, druids, shamans, all believers in the powers of nature. Did one of them write, *Isis lives*?

A bug that looks like a Chinese pea pod with legs darts in front of her. Startled, Poppy jumps, stares at the grey tree trunk, at the other trees that form a narrow thicket between the path and the river, and, carried away by the thin, early morning light, the cool air, the etched name on the grey bark, she loses herself. Her feet no longer touch Mother Earth, she dissolves in the new morning, in the stately trees, in the distant bird cries. She's no longer Poppy, but a broader being, a more abstract, a more harmonious entity.

Just a flash, but she's lifted.

Isis has put out a hand and raised her.

She's no different than those pagans on the mailing list. A remnant from prehistory. She could rename herself Diotima, study the "law of threefold": what you do, good or evil, returns to you three times.

First, she'll take a botany class.

Another hour and she arrives at Swain's Lock. Families and joggers and dogs pass her every two minutes now. Sunday morning on the C & O canal. So many amiable family groups: father, mother, son, daughter, dog. Will she ever be part of such a configuration? For the near future, it looks like it's going to be just her and Metro.

And her botany books.

Damn that Vic! Why no forwarding address? Why so total a disappearance?

The idea doesn't come to her until she's back at her mother's house, helping put in annuals. Her mother's six flats of impatiens will form a sash of color across the front of her house. As Poppy kneels, digging holes for the plants, she uncovers an earthworm that slithers off and disappears.

Like Vic.

Like those kids Abel Moore tracked.

That's it! She'll ask Abel Moore. Provide him an object that belonged to Vic—the elephant hair bracelet?—and see if he can locate him.

All day she considers her plan. She calls Opal (no answer) and Geneva (line disconnected) to discuss it. Why is Geneva's line disconnected?

She finds out that evening when Geneva calls to tell about the fire. Amazed, Poppy drops the spoon she's stirring her coffee with.

"What's that?" Geneva asks.

"I dropped my spoon."

"Drop a spoon, love will come soon."

"Right." Poppy picks up the spoon and reveals her plan to ask Abel Moore's help in tracking down the missing Vic.

AT EIGHT A.M. Sunday morning Opal pokes her head into Sol's study and sniffs. Oil paint. The vaporizer in the middle of the floor. Sol sprawled in sleep. Wearing that ratty brown sweater he should have donated to Goodwill five years ago. Wearing sheepskin slippers!

Sixth night on the sofa.

Which means?

Impossible to guess, so why speculate? She redirects her thoughts to breakfast. In the refrigerator she finds half an avocado (good cholesterol), which she slices and spreads on French bread. She reheats a cup of yesterday's coffee, retrieves the paper from the front lawn, glances at the headlines and the magazine. Will her life improve if she spends an hour reading the paper? If something critical happens, won't someone tell her? If an earthquake occurs, if the end of the world comes, isn't she sure to hear?

End of the world stories for the *Review*? The reverse? Stories about beginnings. Not beginnings of the world, but lesser beginnings. Egyptians begin their year at the autumnal equinox. Greeks begin theirs at summer solstice. Druids started the year on November 1. A good writer could work it up.

The phone rings.

"Guess what?" Zach asks.

"What?"

"Someone found my wallet."

"Good! Good! Good!"

"Guy picked it up from the road. My friend's number was inside."

"You got everything back?"

"People are more honest in the Midwest."

"It doesn't hurt to be lucky."

"One other thing. I think I've fallen in love."

"When did you find time for that?"

"Last night."

"Are we talking about Cindy?"

"Cindy's in California, I'm in Colorado. Her name's Chanel and she has two kids."

"Two kids!"

"They're three and six."

"Kids are a big responsibility."

"Why? They're not my kids."

"Where did you meet her?"

"At a party. That's all I do. Work and party."

"Tough life."

"I might be in the market for an engagement ring."

"Won't it be a little inconvenient with you living here and Chanel living out there?"

"I might relocate."

"You're moving pretty fast from a first date to thinking about en-gagement rings."

"I'm an impulsive kind of guy."

"I won't argue with that."

"Only in my personal life. At work, I'm steady as a rock."

"When do you come back?"

"Tomorrow. My car's at the airport, so I don't need anyone to pick me up."

"Sorry you missed the lecture."

"What did he talk about?"

"The inner life of objects."

"Is that like when the moon stares in my window in a malevolent way?"

"Well—"

"Is the moon an object?"

"A natural object."

"Sometimes my car deliberately stalls."

"Right."

"Gotta go. I'll stop by when I get back."

"See you then."

Article topics. Beginnings. Mazes. Exotic Animals in Big Cities. Pre-Columbian African Influences in the New World. People Who Can't Wear Wristwatches. The Inner Life of Objects.

What did Zach mean by the moon staring at him in a malevolent way? A joke? He's depressed? Feels threatened?

Why doesn't she know these things? She's thoughtless? Doesn't pay attention? Is lack of attention the reason she failed to remember Sol's injured elbow?

She sticks her head once more into Sol's study, but her impatience fails to rouse him. She brews a cup of green tea (one cup of coffee's her limit), drinks it slowly, scribbles a note to Sol and drives to the Georgetown flea market.

At ten A.M. the market's in full swing. The sky's an eye shadow blue (covering up what?) and the mild air seems an invisible net that holds the world together yet allows its particulars to slip through and disappear.

Opal joins the shoppers strolling from table to table, watches as they turn objects upside down to check their prices, bargain, make jokes. The meaning of these odds and ends? Castoffs. Remnants. Rejects. She's traipsing through a vast still life, a landscape shimmering with discards. An oak dresser, missing a few knobs. A Chinese cabinet with a broken hinge.

Both need restoration.

Everywhere, old and imperfect items. Cracked and reglued porcelain figurines. Frayed carpets. Dog-eared magazines.

She slips on her glasses and the objects sharpen into focus. A jar of old-fashioned hat pins. Virginia Woolf's *The Waves*, sans cover. A scratched Plexiglas ashtray with an embedded piece of black lung to encourage people to stop smoking.

Perfect for Zach.

She pays three dollars for it.

Most objects flawed. A Barbie doll with half her hair ripped out. For a few months, during her reconstruction, she identified with Barbie. Like the skinny doll, she'd managed without a nipple. A later procedure remedied the situation.

No one's perfect.

She could be in Sol's garage to the tenth power. A wooden flamingo, its turquoise paint faded. A stained lace tablecloth. A pair of foxed prints. A tarnished soup ladle. A dented candlestick.

Does each imperfect object have a soul?

She spots a small black electric fan that looks like a spider. Her parents owned one like it fifty years ago.

"Does it work?" she asks the vendor who's wearing a cowboy hat.

"Switch is bad."

An unsteady feeling invades her stomach. A bad switch. What would Sol say? That he could fix it. Fixed, it might come in handy. Zach might need it. During a heat wave, an organization looking for fans for the elderly might need it.

She picks up a round breadboard marked 1895 which costs thirty-five dollars. How do they determine it was made in 1895? Rosalie could tell her not only this breadboard's date of manufacture, but also its place of origin, the kind of wood it's made from.

Rosalie once mentioned she's a thing person, not a people person.

Objects speak to Rosalie and Sol, but not to her.

Why is that?

What did Mr. Koldaro say? *You must learn to transfigure an object from something that's coldly reasoned into something that's warmly felt. Pick up a pillow. Handle it as if it's a baby and you're a strict mother. Now pretend you're an inexperienced babysitter. Now you're that baby's bachelor uncle. See the difference! Now pick up the pillow again. This time it's a pumpkin. Treat it like a pumpkin! Now it's a time bomb. A fish you've just caught. A tureen of hot soup.*

An exercise at which she never excelled.

At another table she opens a black lacquer jewelry box with mother-of-pearl palm trees on the lid and a crack along one side. She owned a similar box in high school, where she kept her rhinestone earrings that she wore to the senior prom where they played "When I Fall in Love."

A record she listened to dozens of times.

She hums the tune.

Nat King Cole sang it.

She thumps a faded ceramic vase. At a table covered with books, she scans titles. This vendor also sells records, cassettes, CDs, and sheet music. Music drifts from a van that's parked in the back. She stops, hoping to hear Nat King Cole sing "When I Fall in Love," hoping that what she's thinking the universal mind is also thinking.

But the universal mind remains silent. The music streaming from the van is jazzy, Latin, and unfamiliar.

The natural laws remain unsubverted.

Before her mother and Rosalie moved into their condominium, they sold the house they'd lived in for decades. The shift to smaller quarters meant they had much to dispose of. Opal flew down to help Rosalie sort and organize.

In one box, she uncovered a photograph of herself sitting in Rosalie's lap, a picture she hadn't seen for fifty years. She felt she'd snatched a morsel of cake from a bakery sample tray and now hungered for more. For a week, she sorted photographs, old letters (one she'd written to her father), old clothes (including two beaded flapper-era dresses of her mother's, carefully preserved in tissue paper). Objects galore. A few art-deco pins. A bronze dog. A wall hanging of a hunting scene. *Take what you want*, Rosalie invited. *What's left I'll sell through the shop.*

Opal selected some photos, some wineglasses, a lamp, a cigarette box shaped liked a turtle, although she no longer smoked. Twelve tiny silver spoons. Just below the surface, the life she'd lived more than fifty years ago quivered. It was like a slumbering giant that stirred in its sleep. And if it awoke? If past became present? If the cigarette box in the shape of a turtle carried her back? If the miniature coffee spoons stirred demitasses that spilled into floods and carried her back?

But she didn't want to go back.

You look to the future, I look to the past, Sol said.

She packed up a few boxes, left the rest to Rosalie.

At home, she finds Sol drinking yesterday's coffee and reading the paper. "Worked all night," he says, as he refolds the sports section. "What do you say to a picnic? We could pick up some cheese and bread. Raspberry pastries. A jug of wine."

"Jug of wine?"

"Bottle of ginger ale?"

At Fletcher's Boathouse, they choose a table close to the river. Driftwood from a recent flood is scattered around, and another band of picnickers, a Vietnamese family, are barbecuing. Their three delicate children play horse with sticks of the driftwood.

Across the river lies Virginia.

Opal watches two fishermen set down their tackle boxes and cast their lines. Their spaniel hesitates a moment, then plunges into the water.

After lunch, when Opal's eyes start to feel heavy, she lowers her head onto the picnic table, like a child in grade school, and dozes off. A few minutes later, she awakes and sees Sol engrossed in the travel section of the paper.

"Here's an ad for a cruise to Alaska that concentrates on wildlife," he says.

"Alaska!"

"That doctor I saw is off to the South China Sea."

"Too far."

Sol folds the newspaper. "Know what I'd like to see? Those Indian mounds in the Midwest. Not much is known about the people who built them, but their city was once the biggest in North America."

Opal's fully awake now. Mounds. The Midwest. What's he talking about?

"Their culture had disappeared by the time of Columbus. They only left the mounds."

There's a light in his eyes she recognizes. She can tell she's in for it. "Where exactly are these mounds?" she asks.

"Illinois. On the Mississippi River. About a hundred of them."

"A hundred mounds!"

"They're like pyramids. But flat-topped. The inhabitants carried in dirt and built them up like layer cakes."

"No one knows who built them?"

"Only that they were an advanced culture that flourished around seven hundred A.D. They grew corn and squash and fashioned axes, but without the wheel and draft animals."

"I wouldn't mind seeing them." A low-key car trip across the country. Climb prehistoric weed-covered mounds, poke around for shards from a forgotten world. She adds, "Then we could swing south and visit Houston."

A canoe glides by. The Vietnamese children, straddling a rock overhanging the river, shout at the occupants. A snatch of music, from a passing powerboat, momentarily interrupts the quiet.

"Why Houston?"

"There's a shrine to Eleanor Roosevelt in a city dump down there."

At home they consult a map and figure out mileage.

That evening Opal calls Geneva (line out of order—which means?) and Poppy, who tells her about the fire and gives her Brenda Lovejoy's number. Poppy also mentions that she's not going to marry Russell (not in love) and that she intends to take a botany class in the fall.

"Botany class!" Opal exclaims. "I've read about a garden where vegetal spirits influenced the growth of gigantic flowers and vegetables."

"Vegetal spirits!"

"I'll find out for you. The *Review* could use an article on supernaturally assisted plants."

Poppy promises to consider it.

After Opal dials Brenda's number and listens to Geneva's account of the fire, she offers her house while she and Sol drive west. When Geneva mentions George Bluestone and his research into Arthur Conan Doyle, Opal says, "Do you think he'd let us publish an extract of what he's working on?"

"I'll ask him."

"One other thing. Would you consider writing an article on Yeats? Not a scholarly article on the poetry but a biographical one on Yeats' involvement in the supernatural?"

Geneva promises she will. Once the dust settles.

That night, Opal glances at the pad next to Sol's painting—which is looking more finished—and finds scrawled there, "Greetings from the other side."

"Did you write this?" she asks Sol.

"Would I do a thing like that?"

"Very funny." She rips the slip of paper off and crumples it. But later she smoothes it out and examines it.

Sol stashes his brushes in a can of turpentine at 10:30 P.M. and goes upstairs.

ABEL MOORE STARES out the airplane window at the blue and cloudless sky. Mission accomplished. He'd pulled it off. He didn't try too hard. He got the essence right, if not every detail. He'll be home by early afternoon. In time to drive to the lake for an hour of fishing.

No one assumed he was nuts. A few off-the-wall questions (what are disappearing stars?) but no hostile ones. Nobody asked: Why could you locate thirty-six children, but not the others? A bonafide question. Nobody pressed the point: Why do the gifts of most psychics decline over time? He wouldn't mind knowing the answer to that one either.

He'd dipped into the well and found the water clear. No law against being lucky. Corn can't grow on the ceiling; still, he'd reached up and pulled down an ear.

A check for a thousand dollars. A good dinner. An evening in the spotlight. His luck had held. The root grew deep; the winds of disbelief never touched it.

The whole world believes, if only in snatches. Someone boils water and a flicker of hope billows up in the steam. A dream escapes from the shadow of a trout. Forty-three percent of Americans claim they've experienced a psi episode. Among churchgoers, it's fifty-six percent.

Which proves?

It's important to keep your eye on the ball.

Abel Moore shifts in his seat and reaches for the air conditioning nozzle to adjust the airflow. It's stuffy in here. The young man in the next seat—he's got thinning hair and wears a yellow tie—glances at him.

He's reading a newspaper.

Abel Moore manages a noncommittal smile.

When he's "on," he can "read" an object as accurately as his seatmate reads that newspaper. As accurately as a bloodhound reads a scent. An object has its history embedded in it, encoded in it (sort of like its DNA). The trick's to decipher it. Interpret it. Every object's a Rosetta stone awaiting its translator. But the timing has to be right. It's like moonlight at dawn. Easy to miss.

He'd been "on" in Washington. That old guy's eyeglasses. Geneva Lamb's key ring. Book behind the filing cabinet. Fifty-fifty she'll find one there. No earth-shaking data involved. A few inconsistencies, a few truths. No sun without a shadow. Not perfect but close. As if he had a pipeline to some higher power—as if he really were a Man of Hoodoo. Which he's not. He's a retired auto glass salesman, a widower, given to lucky guesses. The best that can be said about him is that he's not an imitator. He hasn't tried to build a house inside a house. The worst that can be said?

But why dwell on the negative? Geneva seemed receptive to his lunch suggestion. Surprised. She's too young. Everyone's too young.

He sighs, and his seatmate flicks him an interested glance. But Abel Moore turns to the window and stares out.

He's got nothing to say to anyone.

He'd been "on" with that young girl too. Poppy. Poppy and her goddess of a thousand names. Younger than Deb, but a fire inside her. Poppy. Flowers. Plants. A connection there. Like her name. Women less predictable than they were thirty years ago, but the world moves on. Old rules forgotten or brushed aside. Look at Deb. He never dreamed she'd move three thousand miles away and drown herself in her career.

Later in the summer, he might visit her. If her schedule permits.

And Opal.

His mirror image.

He'd been "on." That was paramount. After six arid months, last night his powers returned. An elated feeling, like spotting a flock of goldfinches overhead. Not a force he could restrain or compel. A force that escaped the tangle of his thoughts. Didn't that happen to Daniel Douglass Home, the nineteenth-century psychic? His powers deserted him for a year, then returned. The way a tennis player's serve sometimes deserts him.

Tomorrow a full day. The Institute at nine. Letters to answer. Arrangements to make for the conference in Monterey. The normal hullabaloo. But in the evening, he'll return to an empty house, switch on the TV to submerge the silence.

After the conference he could fly to Seattle and visit Deb. Catch up with her life. Reintroduce her to her rewired father.

He feels sleepy and allows his heavy-lidded eyes to close.

He dozes until a tap on the shoulder arouses him.

"Lunch," Yellow Tie announces.

"Thanks." Abel Moore yawns, rubs his eyes, unlatches the folding tray from the back of the seat in front of him. Lunch consists of sandwiches, roast beef and cheese, a salad, custard. They eat in companionable silence for a minute before the young man volunteers, "I'm a freelance journalist. Flying to Jacksonville for an interview."

"What kind of interview?"

"With a famous man. If he'll see me."

"A long way to fly if he won't."

"You said it." The young man spreads mustard on his sandwich in an emphatic way.

"What if he won't?" Suddenly Abel Moore's curious.

"I'll make him an irresistible offer."

Money no doubt, but since it's impolite to mention it, a change of subject is in order. "Washington your home?"

"Pittsburgh. How about you? You live in Washington?"

Abel Moore shakes his head. "Flew up for a lecture."

"Anyone I've heard of?"

"Doubt it. Man called Abel Moore."

"Abel Moore!" Yellow Tie sits up so suddenly his knees knock against his tray. "That's the guy I hope to interview in Jacksonville!"

Abel Moore loosens his tie. "What a coincidence." This must be what it's like to witness your own funeral.

"I wish I'd heard it. Did he talk about psychometry? That nature is full of daguerreotypes of past events?"

"Something like that."

"Do you believe it? I mean, does it make sense to you?"

Abel Moore wipes his mouth with his napkin. "I'm not sure it makes sense, but I believe it."

"I'd like to believe it," Yellow Tie says.

"Why is that?"

The young man shrugs. "Hard to say. One wants to believe." He shifts in his seat and adds, "There's a personal reason too."

"Ah."

"It's a long story."

Abel Moore knows he's going to hear it, but so be it. What else does he have to do? He finishes his custard, leans back. A steward rolls a food cart down the aisle, offering coffee. Both Abel Moore and the young man extend their cups.

"My great-great-uncle—on my mother's side—was a geologist and an explorer. I'm named after him. Hillis Myers."

"Nice to meet you, Mr. Myers," Abel Moore mumbles, hoping his seatmate won't notice he fails to provide his own name.

He doesn't seem to, and continues his story. "Uncle Hillis was a geologist. About a hundred years ago he signed on a ship called the *Rose of Sharon*, which set out to collect animal, vegetable, and mineral specimens. He was the mineral guy. They sailed south to South America, around Cape Horn and up the coasts of Chile and Peru, mapping and collecting specimens, often stopping for weeks at certain sites to gather and catalogue their samples. Like Darwin's expedition to the Galápagos, Uncle Hillis' voyage lasted three years."

"Go on." Abel Moore closes his eyes, listens.

"While on the expedition, Uncle Hillis discovered a rich gold deposit which he noted in his journal. In the effects found after his death, there were rocks with wide veins of gold that have been verified as eighty-two percent pyrite, an indication of a rich lode. Uncle Hillis, according to family lore, meant to return and mine the deposit after the expedition finished."

"But he never did," Abel Moore guesses.

"Never got around to it. He married and raised a family. For decades he worked for the U.S. Geological Survey in Wyoming and Utah. He often mentioned that one day he'd go back."

Abel Moore can guess where all this is leading but sits silently, eyes closed, listening.

"He was a respected geologist, not a crazy prospector. He didn't leave a map, only the ore samples."

"A pity."

"We have a box of those samples," Yellow Tie says. "And this Abel Moore's a psychometrist. Objects 'speak' to him. They showed him a baseball glove once, and he was able to track its owner in another city."

"I read about that."

"If I could convince Abel Moore to concentrate on Uncle Hillis' specimens, maybe he could figure out where they came from."

"South America's a big place."

"I know. It's probably a pipe dream, but I'd like to outfit a small expedition. Me. Abel Moore. One or two others who know about geology and mining."

"You'd want Abel Moore to go along?"

"We need him to pinpoint the site. Don't you think he'd have a better shot if he went down there?"

"Sometimes his powers don't work. What if he misdirects you?"

"A risk. But less chance if he's with us, right? My philosophy is: Nothing ventured, nothing gained. All Abel Moore has to lose is a few weeks of his time."

"A few weeks—"

"The first expedition would be a preliminary survey. Find the location. Scout the area. Establish we're not encroaching on anybody's property, secure permits if we need them. Everything on the up and up. Determine there are no hostile tribes. Even do a little fishing."

"Fishing!"

"Great rivers down there."

"An amazing plan. When would you expect to go? If you succeed in interesting Abel Moore."

"In a few months. What do you think? If you were Abel Moore, would it interest you?"

"Hard to say."

"First thing tomorrow, I'm going to try to sell the whole package. Ore samples, jungle trek, partnership in a gold mine."

Abel Moore sips his coffee. Partnership in a gold mine! Fishing and hiking! Would his powers be in working order? No way to predict. Effort and good intentions don't mean a thing. Desire for personal gain has wrecked the powers of many a psychic. It's best, like the chrysanthemum, to desire nothing. Still, he'd been "on" last night. He might be "on" with the ore samples. No law against being lucky. Hasn't he been sitting in an office too long? Lecturing. Conducting workshops. A trip to South America! Fish those rivers. Watch the constellations from a forest camp. Let his spirit uncoil to the corners of the earth. He'll need shots, sturdy boots.

Hillis Myers interrupts this daydream. "What do you think? Have I got a chance?"

"Why not?" Abel Moore says. "Why not?"

And suddenly he can't wait for tomorrow morning when Hillis Myers will walk into his office at the Institute and realize who he'd been talking to. He glances at the young man who's smiling in a self-satisfied way. Which prompts Abel Moore to consider that maybe Myers has known all along who he is.

Either way, an interesting prospect.

ACKNOWLEDGMENT OF SOURCES

The work of Yeats is reprinted with the permission of Simon & Schuster from *THE POEMS OF W.B. YEATS: A NEW EDITION*, edited by Richard J. Finneran (New York: Macmillan, 1983).

The Inner Life of Objects is a work of fiction, and some books (such as *Borderlines*), magazines, and other work mentioned in the text are fictional. Among the many sources that provided information for this book, grateful acknowledgment is made for the following: Charles McGaw's *Acting Is Believing: A Basic Method* (New York: Holt, Rinehart and Winston, 1975, 3rd edition). Mario's Conservation Services for the Decorative Arts. "I-Control-Me-Person," Bernard Asbell's *Book of You* (New York: Ballantine Books/A Fawcett Columbine Book, 1991). Information about Isis and other goddesses was derived from Barbara G. Walker's *The Woman's Encyclopedia of Myths and Secrets* (New York: Harper Collins Publishers, Inc., 1983). Information for the fictional book *A History of Women in America* and other discussion of women's history was derived from Sheila M. Rothman's *Woman's Proper Place* (New York: Basic Books, Inc., 1978) and Judy Chicago's *The Dinner Party* (Garden City, NY: Anchor Press/Doubleday, 1979), among others. Information about morphic fields was derived from David Jay Brown and Rebecca McClean Novick's "What the Universe Remembers: An Interview with Rupert Sheldrake," *The Sun: A Magazine of Ideas* (July 1993). Information about capabilities of consciousness of humans and animals is derived from Barbara B. Brown's *Supermind* (New York: Bantam Books, 1983).

About the
Author

MAXINE COMBS' previous books include *Handbook of the Strange* (Signal Books, 1996), a novella and collection of interrelated stories; *The Foam of Perilous Seas* (Slough Press, 1990), a chapbook of fiction; and *Swimming Out of the Collective Unconscious* (Wineberry Press, 1989), a chapbook of poetry. She moved to Washington, D.C., in the early 1970s, where she taught English at several local universities and began publishing fiction, poetry, and reviews in small press journals. In 1998 she won the Larry Neal Award for Fiction and in 1990 received the Slough Press Fiction Award. She is a fiction editor for *The Antietam Review* and has received grants from the D.C. Commission on the Arts and Humanities and the National Endowment for the Arts and from the Virginia Center for the Creative Arts. She lives with her husband in Washington, D.C.

Colophon

The text of this book was composed in Goudy
with titles in Smack.
Page layout and composition provided by
ImPrint Services, Corvallis, Oregon.